January Fiftee

ALSO BY RACHEL SWIRSKY

How the World Became Quiet

Through the Drowsy Dark

JANUARY FIFTEENTH

RACHEL SWIRSKY

A TOM DOHERTY ASSOCIATES BOOK

NEW YORK

This is a work of fiction. All of the characters, organizations, and events portrayed in this novella are either products of the author's imagination or are used fictitiously.

JANUARY FIFTEENTH

Edited by Jonathan Strahan

Cover photograph © Getty Images
Cover design by Christine Foltzer

A Tordotcom Book
Published by Tom Doherty Associates
120 Broadway
New York, NY 10271

www.tor.com

ISBN 978-1-250-19893-8 (ebook)
ISBN 978-1-250-19894-5 (trade paperback)

First Edition: 2022

To my parents, Lyle Merithew and Sandy Swirsky, with extra and emphatic thanks for their support while I was writing this book.

Author's Note

January Fifteenth takes place in a near-future United States of America with a Universal Basic Income (UBI) program. If you're not familiar with the term, Universal Basic Income is a policy proposal for the government to provide an annual income to its citizens. Details vary—like how much that income should be—but every citizen would get it, without condition.

For me at least, any argument about UBI begins with one question: Will it help people?

Practical assessment follows, of course, but that's the first thing we have to know. In its ideal form, if everything went perfectly, would UBI improve people's lives? I don't have a definitive answer, although I pose a series of possible questions and answers in this novella.

During my research on US UBI proposals, most of the hypotheticals I saw concentrated on the traditional concerns of the right versus left political axis. Would UBI open new possibilities for society or encourage a culture of laziness and dependency?

I became more curious about other questions. For instance, some people dislike that UBI goes to people of any social class—so what might (some) rich kids do with it? Some people are wary about the ways cults exploit contemporary welfare programs—what might they do with UBI, and how might others try to stop them? Pervasive, systemic racism has created an enormous disparity between the assets of Black and White American households—can and should we brush over that history as if Black and White communities have an equal starting point? Money can help someone escape an abusive relationship, but would Universal Basic Income change what happens afterward?

The characters in this book have gone through hard things, from being orphaned to domestic violence to forced marriage. Many of the scenarios in this book reflect situations that I or people close to me have gone through. Others evolved through research and talking to people. So many of us have gone through similar tribulations, whether the more common horrors like casual racism and sexual assault, or the more rarefied ones like cult exploitation. These things impact our lives. They affect our happiness. They certainly affect how and why Universal Basic Income could change our circumstances.

Although I hope *January Fifteenth* is true to the characters and emotions, I can't claim it's an accurate prediction. UBI could play out in lots of ways that are equally, if not more, plausible. For example, in *January Fifteenth,* the practical side of running UBI is relatively smooth and easy. That choice allows me to let fiddly details fade into the background while I focus on the characters. But is it the most likely scenario? Probably not—very few things seem to be easy.

Even within the world I set up, there are a ton of possible alternative and conflicting scenarios. I could have happily kept adding more. In fact, a fifth thread ended up on the cutting room floor during an early draft when the word count kept relentlessly increasing.

If I can make any "true" predictions, I suppose they are these:

1. Money can make life easier, but it can't solve everything.
2. Adding money to a system with underlying problems won't fix those problems on its own.
3. After any massive change, some people will be better off, some people will be worse off, and many people will be both better and worse off.
4. However the future unfolds, it won't go according to my values. There will always be outcomes I don't expect. Some of them will contradict my beliefs about the world.
5. I'm definitely wrong about something.

UBI DAY: EARLY

Hannah

The blizzard first touched land in Maine. It glazed lakes and lighthouses and red-shingled roofs, and billowed through naked ash trees. It chased coastal waves southward to New Hampshire and then moved inland through Concord and into upstate New York, past Saratoga Springs and Syracuse. In Canastota, the historic Erie Canal froze beside iced railroad tracks, neither taking anyone anywhere.

Hannah Klopfer felt grateful once again that she and the boys had been able to find a furnished rental inside their budget that was within easy walking distance of necessities like the post office and the grocery store. She zipped up her down jacket and tugged her hat over her ears. She patted her pockets: wallet, phone, keys. As she grabbed her scarf from the aging brass rack by the door, it made a shuddery twang against the greasy metal.

As the twanging faded, Hannah heard a distant, quiet shuffle from the back of the house. Something wooden groaned. Hannah's mouth went dry. The ends of her scarf dropped from her hands, unwound, and fell loosely across her chest.

Her heart pounded. She hadn't expected Abigail to find them so fast. She took a deep breath to shout upstairs for Jake and Isaiah to start piling furniture against their bedroom door.

A high-pitched giggle broke the quiet, followed by another. Hannah exhaled in relief. Thank God. It was just the boys playing.

Her heart hadn't stopped pounding, though. Damn it. *Damn it!* What was she supposed to do when the boys *wouldn't listen*? This wasn't about sticking their fingers in their cereal or getting crayon on the walls. Did it really matter that it was developmentally normal for a seven-year-old to test authority if it ended up giving Abigail a way back into their lives?

God forbid, what if Abigail came with a gun? People shot their exes and their kids all the time. Hannah didn't think Abigail would do something like that—but at one point, Hannah had believed Abigail would never hurt her, and then she'd believed Abigail would never hurt the kids, and there were only so many times she could be wrong before she realized her instincts were bullshit.

She scanned the front room. Despite being crammed awkwardly between the kitchen and the stairs, it was full of places for kids to hide among the crowded armchairs, end tables, and obsolete music systems. The landlady stored her cartoon-themed collectables on motley bookcases; the figures cast weird, elongated shadows shaped like rabbit ears and dynamite.

"Hey, Jake! Isaiah! Where are you?" Hannah called.

There was a lot of silence. *Don't shout,* Hannah told herself.

There was another little giggle, followed by, "Shh!"

She told herself, *Don't cry. They don't need to know how scared you are.*

She breathed to calm herself, and then did it again. Her voice was scratchy. "Okay, dudes, for the next five minutes, I'm willing to believe you two were transported down here by aliens." She waited a second for them to answer. "Or fell through a tunnel under the bunk bed." She gave it one more try. "Or you've been sleepwalking until this very second."

There wasn't even a giggle this time. Jake was getting better at herding his little brother.

"Please?" Hannah's voice broke. "Come on, Jake, we've talked about this. Isaiah only does things like this if his big brother does it first. Don't you want to be a better big brother?"

No, damn it, that was shaming, not helping. Kids could be crushed so easily. They picked up on things you didn't even know you'd dropped.

She tried again. She didn't mean her tone to be so sharp; she really didn't. She was just scared. "I *need* you to be a better brother. You'll get him hurt."

That was worse.

Still, it coaxed Jake out from between a love seat and a record player, leading his brother, Isaiah, by the hand.

Resentfully, he said, "It was . . . j-just a game." His lip wobbled; he began to cry. His emotions were so big right now, and changed so fast. "Mama, I'm sorry, Mama. Mama! I'll be—better—I wa-want—to be good—"

He was so anxious to please. It broke her heart in pieces.

She crushed Jake into a hug, scooping Isaiah in with them. Their arms compressed her down jacket with a comforting wintery sound.

She said, "You're good. You're good enough. I'm sorry, Jake. You're only seven. You shouldn't have to worry ab—" She cut herself off before she could finish the sentence, scolding herself for almost scaring them again. There had to be another way to get them to listen than talking about nightmare scenarios. "I know it's fun to break rules. It's funny to trick me. But you can't, Jake. I'm so sorry. Okay? I'll tell you a rule tomorrow you can break. Play with your food or color on the walls or—" She gestured helplessly. "Just take care of Isaiah for me today, okay? Just be good today. Go up to your room and stay there, and you can play if you don't make any noise, but I need you to stay there, and I need you to listen to anything I say, okay? Okay? And if someone else comes in the house, pile furniture against your door like we practiced. Okay?"

Sniffing and snuffling, Jake nodded, and wiped his nose with the back of his hand.

Isaiah looked up at Hannah with his enormous blue eyes. "Mama, I don't want to see Mom."

People spent so much time trying to make sure their kids were precocious, but when you had kids with intuition like heat-seeking missiles, how were you supposed to protect them?

Hannah said, "I know, honey, I don't want to see Abigail either." She coughed to cover the break in her voice. "Jake, will you take your brother back upstairs? Either of you need to pee?" When neither spoke, she continued, "Good. Go straight up. Close the door, and don't open it again until I say it's okay. It's important, remember? Okay . . ." she said, exhaling and trying to calm down. "Okay, okay. I'll be back real soon."

She watched the boys go upstairs as she wrapped the scarf around her neck. The old steps were so steep, they could almost be a ladder. Jake ran them at full speed, knees going up and down like pistons. Isaiah's awkward little hop from step to step made Hannah ache to grab him and carry him upstairs in her arms—but he preferred his own feet, and she had to leave anyway.

Janelle

West of Canastota, New York, the storm skulked across the Finger Lakes, too grumpy to decide between rain and snow. It pushed restless and sullen waves westward across Lake Michigan before taking land again as a wintry mix that turned to slush on the Chicago streets.

Somewhere around Revere Park, one of Janelle Butler's buzzcams started acting up. The thing was finicky about the cold. It was supposed to be top-notch, but Janelle hadn't found any difference between brands. Top or bottom dollar, freelance reporters got screwed.

She didn't need this. January was bad enough with the endless demands from news aggregators asking for the same, repetitive Universal Basic Income stories. It had been interesting to go around and ask the man, woman, and child on the street how they felt about UBI when the program started. Since then the aggregators had been sending her out every year to do the same old interviews and wear out the same old questions that someone else had already worn out, earlier and probably better.

She felt like a bee doing the same mindless tasks year

after year, just like all the other bees. Get the honey. Do a dance. Interview someone who thinks her cats should get UBI.

Interview a violinist who uses their money to fund lessons for disadvantaged kids. Interview a new mom about the savings fund she set aside for her baby. Interview a lawyer representing a class action lawsuit against a landlord for extorting his tenant's disbursements. Interview a senior citizen who lost his home because of problems with the transition from social security. Interview the protestors wherever they are this year. Interview the protestors protesting the other protestors wherever they are this year.

The stories weren't all terrible. Her legitimate, non-cynical, favorite piece had been "interview an ex-con who spent her UBI on land and a trailer so she can live off the grid and make pots." Interesting, specific, quirky. Of course, that had been the first year—and of course, none of the aggregators had ever wanted a follow-up. Still, Janelle and Dynasty had clicked, and Janelle called her up for a chat every UBI Day. So, hey, her job had been good for something at least once. And it was something to look forward to after all the boring interviews were done.

It occurred to Janelle, not for the first time, that the aggregators would probably love to run her story too, if she wedged it into the right box. Sentimental: Chicago-based twenty-eight-year-old raises fourteen-year-old sister after parents die in plane crash. Political: Former activist relies on legislation she championed to care for orphaned sibling. Socially responsible: UBI keeps Black families together.

Anyway. The upshot was that there was always work for two weeks in January, even if you didn't have a great relationship with the major aggregators. A lot of the year was hit-or-miss. UBI stories were a pillar of her income.

So of course one of her buzzcams was broken.

On the porch of the very fancy home where she was supposed to conduct her next interview—heterosexual couple Carinna and August, married eleven years—she banged, tapped, cursed, and cajoled the cam at increasing volume. Finally, it sputtered awake like a sulky teenager, emitted a grinding screech, and lit up. She touched the pendant cross she wore around her neck in brief thanks.

The obstreperous buzzcam and its twin gave their signature cicada-like whine as she set them to record. They rose to hover over her shoulders. Both of them jittered, even the one that was theoretically in fine working order.

She put on her "Hello! I'm nice and you should open up to me about interesting things!" smile, and hoped her interviewees hadn't heard her swearing through the door.

The White woman who answered wore a loose long-sleeved navy jumpsuit from a fancy brand. A bit of wear at the seams suggested she might only have a few $3,000 outfits instead of whole racks. Most of her jewelry managed the trick of sophistication through modesty, except for the diamond in her wedding ring which was definitely a braggart. She wore her hair skinned back into a tight bun at her nape. She had a bottle of wine in one hand, as if she'd been interrupted in the middle of entertaining. People had weird ideas about what they wanted to be found doing on camera.

"Sorry, I was reorganizing the wine rack," said Carinna.

"Don't worry, they probably won't use this part," Janelle said.

Carinna's face fell for a moment but quickly regained its polish.

She led Janelle into the front room where the modernist leather furniture showed a few scuffs. The fireplace with the marble tile looked like it hadn't been used very much. Her husband, August, turned out to be Black, which a cynical part of Janelle suggested was why she'd been assigned this particular interview. An open case of cigars sat on the table in front of him. Only one cigar had been taken out.

Oh, the amazing tapestry of the human subconscious. They probably didn't realize they were telegraphing class anxiety with every detail. The wine-and-cigars thing was straight out of old movies about the glamorous upper crust. In Janelle's experience, the richest people actually tended to show off unique hobbies or collections, if they showed off anything.

So, that was Carinna and August: rich, but not as rich as they wanted to be, and feeling put-upon about it. Janelle liked to make bets with herself about what kind of interview she was about to get, but this one was too easy.

Ten minutes later: "—We're not rich, but our taxes just keep going up—"

God, it was going to be a long day.

Janelle was on the train, halfway to her next interview, when a yellow dot flashed in her right eye. She swore at the afterimage. "Motherf—" Somehow, her damn phone had once again managed to switch on the setting to send notifications through her contacts.

"Off, off, off, how do I turn the damn thing off," she muttered to herself, fumbling for her phone in her purse.

The person sitting next to Janelle shuffled their shopping bag in their lap and let out an aggrieved sigh. Janelle suppressed simultaneous urges to apologize and give her one back.

Once she managed to grab the phone, Janelle was shocked to see the message wasn't spam. She thumbed the callback. Her sister, Nevaeh, picked up instantly.

"Heyyyy Janni," Nevaeh said.

The voice blasted on speaker—Janelle had forgotten to change the settings to wavve the sound into her ear. As Janelle clicked through the options menu, the person with the shopping bag groaned.

"What is it?" Janelle asked Nevaeh.

"Why'd you take so long to wavve back?" Nevaeh asked.

"Phone trouble," Janelle grumbled.

"You know calling your wrister a phone makes you sound a million years old."

"It walks like a phone and it quacks like a phone. If I took it to the park, it would paddle about on a pond and eat bread crumbs like a phone. It's a phone."

"They're not the same thing."

"You know what a phone is by any other name? A *phone*."

"It would work better if you'd just *wear* it."

"Why are you calling me in the middle of the day?"

"I'm being sent home."

"What?"

"I'm being sent home."

"From school?"

"Uh, yeah?"

"Why? What did you do?"

"Why did I have to do something?"

"What was it?"

"I didn't *do* anything...." There was a brief pause before Nevaeh added, "You've got to pick me up."

"You're kidding me."

"No. Sorry."

"You know how busy I am today. I don't have time for this."

"Sorry."

Janelle shook her head. "You have to tell them I can't."

"I can try, but I think they'll be upset."

Janelle groaned, trying to mentally reshuffle her schedule. "Are you throwing up or something?"

"Or something."

She sighed with bad grace. "Are there any subs at the office? Does everyone know it'll be me coming, not a parent?"

"Everyone remembers you," Nevaeh said. "I think Mrs. Walker forgot you're my sister, though. She said you look good for your age."

This did not improve Janelle's mood. "I do *not* look like your mom. I'd have been *fourteen*." She rubbed her forehead. "Mrs. Walker—is that the one who keeps calling you Prince?"

"Yeah," Nevaeh said. "She's a little..."

"Transphobic," said Janelle.

"More sort of generally confused. She knows I

changed my name—and I *think* she knows why? But she forgets which name is the right one. She keeps telling me Prince is a cute name for a girl."

Janelle snorted, then made a face. "I want to know why the hell your old name still shows up in their systems at all."

"Prince *could* be a cute name for a girl," Nevaeh said. "I hope Mrs. Walker has a daughter and names her Prince and dresses her in ruffles and a little sash."

Janelle laughed. The train rattled into a station, walls shaking as the brakes shrilled. All her anxieties about money and time reboarded alongside a trio wearing matching yellow plaid blazers.

She checked the map on her phone. "I'll be there in half an hour. Make sure you've got your stuff ready to go."

"Doubtless."

Janelle clicked off the phone, muttering to herself about who she was going to need to contact and what she was going to need to cancel.

The person with the shopping bag made a face and got up to stand on the other side of the car. Janelle mentally tossed them into her "things to ignore" dumpster, along with the circling worries about how much money they weren't going to have for getting through the rest of the year.

Olivia

The storm mellowed as it left Chicago. Dapples of sunlight peeked sporadically through the clouds, giving way to the glare of sun-on-snow before reaching Peoria. In Kansas, the temperature set record highs; people in Topeka went out in short sleeves, complaining that no one could predict the weather anymore.

In Aspen, Colorado, new snow drifted onto thick, perfect powder.

"*Whoop! Whoop!* Waste Day! *Whoop! Whoop!*"

Olivia Latham woke blurrily, her face between a soft, white pillow and the back of a soft, white sofa. She was still a little drunk. Familiar voices blended together as she yawned.

"Whoop! Whoop! Whoooooop!"

"Jesus Christ, Pauline. They should hire you as an ambulance siren."

"Does anyone know where the fuck William is?"

"Wasssste Daaaay! Whoop!"

"Seriously, where the fuck is William?"

It was good to wake up flushed and cozy, surrounded

by friends. The eight of them hadn't been together since high school graduation last year. They were all renting this top-floor suite for a week of winter break as part of the pact they'd made to stay friends in college.

Everyone had flown in last night, and then they'd started drinking right away so Don could show off the cocktails he'd learned at UPenn. Around . . . 4:00 A.M.? Olivia had said she was going to take a nap.

The sun was up now. Pale light came through the huge windows overlooking the slopes. Olivia liked how the snow on some of the mountain crests looked a little bluish. She liked the green lines of the distant trees. The mountains and the snow seemed happy, like they were hanging out on a day that was exactly what winter should be. Cold outside, warm inside. Huge outside, tiny inside. She was just a tiny, little person looking out at the bigness of the world.

Maybe that should have been scary, but the way the world was this morning made it feel okay that she was just something small. She always felt small, but it had gotten so much worse in college.

Don't think about that. Don't think about Brown. Don't think about failing. Don't think about spring semester starting in ten days. Don't think about talking to your parents.

It was so good to be back with high school friends who didn't expect anything from her. Drowsily, she closed her eyes again and listened to the hum of their voices.

Don was doing his charismatic clown routine as he shared drink recipes with Elsa.

"—now, you can make it without the bacon-fat infusion," said Don. "But, my friend! Do not leave out the habanero. You'll regret it if you leave out the habanero."

Elsa answered, "Thank *God.* You do not *understand.* I really *needed* this recipe. Because my roommate brought back all this second-rate mezcal from Oaxaca, and if we *have* to drink it *straight* one more time—"

Katie paced by the window, hand-wavving her new boyfriend at Oxford. "—yeah, when everyone got here, it felt like, *Oh. This is high school again, except that high school is still over. Thank God.*... Yeah, William's here too.... No, he's left me alone so far. He's planning some kind of big thing for everyone today—" Katie's voice broke off, then got louder. "Stop. I can handle my ex. You're making me regret telling you what happened—"

Leroy was still fighting with Freddie. They had ended up at Yale, along with William. The three of them were so lucky to be together.

"What the hell does William even want?" Leroy asked.

"Who knows?" said Fred.

Leroy again: "He got us up at the crack of dawn. This better not be a prank."

Somewhere across the room, Pauline whooped.

Olivia sighed happily. A golden sense of well-being melted through her. She said, "This is nice."

Nobody paid attention.

Leroy kept getting louder. "I spent the whole semester getting up at five in the fucking a.m. every day so I could swim at six. I need my fucking sleep, man."

Freddie said, "Don't yell at me about it. I can't do anything about William."

"Blah, blah, blah, shout, snipe," said Katie. She'd wavved bye to her boyfriend and shut off her wrister. "You two suck so much less when you're dating."

Leroy scoffed.

Freddie said, "Never again."

"Just stop fighting or go somewhere else to do it," said Katie.

"We can't. Because your boyfriend, William the Cocksucker, isn't here," said Leroy.

"Clever," said Katie sarcastically. "Don't call him my boyfriend."

"Yeah, it *is* clever," Leroy said back.

Katie made an exasperated noise and Olivia heard her walking around the sofa. Leroy and Freddie started fighting again. Olivia opened her eyes as Katie came up next to her and offered her a drink.

"Do you want a Fuzzy Navel?" Katie asked.

Olivia giggled.

"Don't worry. It's not actual lint."

Katie handed down the glass. Olivia liked how orange it was, how bright.

Katie continued, "Don's still showing off his bartending. This is peach schnapps and orange juice. He put in some Crystal Head."

Olivia squinted at the drink. "Huh?"

"Crystal Head vodka," said Katie. "It comes in a skull."

Olivia flinched. "What?"

"A glass skull," Katie said, laughing. "It's just a bottle."

"Oh," said Olivia, relieved.

Katie said, "Sorry, didn't mean to scare you."

Olivia brought the drink to her nose to inhale the brightness. She drank a little; fizzy tartness filled her mouth.

"Any good?"

"It tastes like sun," Olivia said.

"I guess that's good?"

Katie flopped next to Olivia on the couch. Her dress was loose and flowing in that way that made really bony girls like Katie look even skinnier. It showed off her collarbone and her wrists and her really, really expensive wrister with its slender Cartier band woven from three colors of gold.

Katie raised her bright yellow drink to gesture behind them. "Can you believe Leroy? I haven't been with

William since junior year. Doesn't it feel like we're back in high school?"

"Yeah. It does," Olivia agreed, smiling.

Katie downed half of her yellow drink at once. Her eyes were red and shiny from who-knew-how-many more she'd had since last night. Her rust-colored ponytail fell in her face. She pushed it aside again.

"I think I always knew our friends weren't very nice," Katie said, "but it's hard to see when you're in it. Even if you want to break free, how can you? It's all fish not knowing the word for water."

Katie looked so sad. Olivia made an *I'm sorry* noise. She sipped more sweet sun.

"You're nice," Katie said. "Everyone else is fucked-up, but you don't play games, Olivia. You don't think like that. I wasted so much time with them in high school. I wish I'd spent more time with you."

Bubbles fizzed pleasantly in Olivia's mouth.

"Don't let them get to you while we're here, okay?" Katie said. "Remember *they're* the assholes."

"Okay."

"And you sh—"

Leroy's sudden shout interrupted them. "I just want to know—where the hell is William?"

"Here the hell is William!" answered William.

Katie and Olivia turned simultaneously to look over

the back of the couch. William was coming into the room, followed by a bunch of strangers.

The newcomers looked like college students. A lot of them were wearing university sweatshirts. Most of them were dressed to lounge, but a few were dressed up, probably from last night's clubbing. Backless shirts on the girls; headbands on the guys; everywhere, splashes of the beautiful, bright lemon yellow that was popular right now.

A group that was already dressed to gear up and ski lined up against the back wall. A blonde girl complained and tried to leave, but the guys she was with kept pulling her back.

By the piano, a pair of femme neuts were playing with each other's hair. Olivia decided she liked their shiny, heeled boots. Her friends didn't hang out with neuts very often. No reason. They just didn't.

Katie tugged fretfully at her ponytail the way she did. She hissed under her breath, "William did *not* ask if it was okay to bring people over."

William looked drunk and wobbly. He was even skinnier than he'd been in high school. The shadows underneath his eyes were huge, like they'd been painted on with makeup. His jacket was vintage plaid, with actual leather patches on the elbows, but it was a lot too small. His jeans were a lot too big. His oxfords were polished, though. William always polished his shoes. He said that shoes were the first thing a lot of people noticed when they met someone, even if they didn't realize they'd glanced down. Therefore, polished shoes could make someone have a good feeling about you without knowing why.

William spread his arms dramatically. "Welcome, everyone! To the best Waste Day party you've ever seen!"

In the kitchen, holding a tequila bottle, Pauline waved her hands in the air. *"Whoop! Whoop! Wasssste Daaaaaaay!"*

Sarah

As the weather moved southwest, it grew warmer until even the ice glazing the dawn grass melted away. Zion National Park was damp and chilly, the canyon empty of tourists to watch the red sandstone turn crimson in the rain.

Near Utah's southern border, women in prairie dresses walked through the drizzle on the shoulder of the highway. They carried infants and sleepy toddlers, and urged older children along. The prophet's women and children trekked on foot every year to protest the state's requirement that they go in-person to collect their benefits. The state claimed it was to mitigate "abuses of the system," but everyone knew it was just another way to harass them for having different beliefs. Many had moved away from Utah to avoid hostile laws, but some of them refused to be bullied out of their homes by heretics.

Sarah Mortar's third-trimester nausea made it difficult to keep up. Everything set it off: the walking, the smell of damp wool, her shoes squishing in the mud. The morning sickness was supposed to be over by now, but of course she'd been one of the lucky few who'd gotten it back in month seven.

Her sister-wives, Faith, Dorcas, and Mary, were slightly ahead of her, walking side by side in step as if they were marching. They were all more than ten years older than Sarah, had spotless reputations, and had not appreciated that the new fifteen-year-old who'd been brought into their house was known as a stubborn loner. Their pace wasn't unreasonable—unless you were pregnant and trying not to throw up. Sarah had been jogging after them at intervals all morning.

Nausea made Sarah grumpy, and being grumpy made it hard to ignore her sister-wives' haranguing. They never quite whispered, but the three of them had a trick of pitching their voices so that only the occasional hushed phrase broke through.

". . . if her brother is anything like she is . . ."

Today, they were talking about her little brother, Toby.

". . . if he's got anything like her mouth . . ."

Toby, who was twelve years old.

". . . hear he's been making trouble for ages . . ."

Toby, who her dad had driven off with three nights ago in the pickup and then left somewhere on the highway.

". . . can't tolerate disrespect forever, can you? . . ."

". . . have some room for the good boys . . ."

". . . as my granny said, they served the deserved!"

Every few minutes, they giggled. *That* was always easy to hear.

Sarah couldn't even distinguish their individual laughter anymore. They were like a brace of geese that wouldn't stop honking. Her own *family* wouldn't talk about Toby anymore, but her sister-wives shrilled and hooted. A desperate twelve-year-old shoving his face against the passenger-side window, blinking blood out of his terrified eyes as the engine revved—how *funny*! Sarah's face got hotter and hotter as she remembered it. She only didn't shout in their stupid faces for them to shut up because her throat had closed with anger.

Nausea overwhelmed her fury and she bent over to heave.

Faith, Dorcas, and Mary were far ahead by the time she was done. They'd probably been waiting for a plausible opportunity to "accidentally" leave her behind.

Good. Better for everyone.

"You cows," she growled under her breath. "You don't know anything about Toby. Don't even talk about him. Don't even *talk* about him!"

Some other women passed with their children. Hopefully they hadn't heard.

She heaved a few more times. It seemed to be over, but she stayed where she was for a bit in case she got a surprise. Looking at the road and thinking about how far there was still to go, Sarah decided she hated whoever had made the law demanding in-person pickup almost as much as she hated her sister-wives.

Before long, without walking to warm her up, Sarah started shivering. She heard someone squishing behind her just before they draped something warm over her shoulders. She turned to see Agnes, her skinny ten-year-old cousin, standing on tiptoe.

"Don't worry," Agnes said. "The sickness'll go away again." She frowned at the road ahead. "It looks like Faith and all went on already."

"I know."

"They probably didn't see you?" Agnes said uncertainly.

Sarah gave a vague shrug. Agnes still believed the nice lies. *Sister-wives keep each other sweet.*

Lies. They were like barbed hooks that got stuck in you and left bloody holes when you ripped them out. You could yank out the ones you found, but there were always more.

All the stupid reasons boys had been sent away kept circling in her mind along with the memory of Toby. It was so dumb, she'd never questioned them before. *Clement paid inappropriate attention to the prophet's wives. Bartholomew listened to outsider music. Toby disrespected his father and refused to do his chores—*

Sarah's hand made an involuntary fist. "We should get

on. Do you want your shawl back?"

Agnes looked pleased with herself for helping. "No, I run hot. Mom says it's some kind of miracle since I'm so skinny."

Sarah wasn't surprised when Agnes fell in to walk beside her. Agnes antagonized most people with her loud, toneless voice and constant talking, so she clung like a monkey to anyone who'd let her. Sarah usually put up with it, but she needed time alone to think.

She had been visiting her father's house for dinner the night they turned out Toby, trying to get away from Faith, Dorcas, and Mary for a few hours. If she hadn't, then she wouldn't have seen her dad drag Toby into the front yard and call for her brothers to get in their punches. She wouldn't keep seeing that image of Toby's face in her mind now. Maybe that would have been better? No, it would have been worse.

She avoided falling into step with Agnes so it wouldn't seem like they were pairing up.

Agnes smelled slightly of wet dog; she must have been playing with one of the mutts. The smell probably wouldn't have bothered Sarah if she hadn't been pregnant, but it didn't help.

Sarah said, "You don't have to walk with me. I'll slow you down."

"Someone should be around in case." Agnes's expression

was extremely serious. "Faith and all must be worried."

Sarah snorted involuntarily.

"Do you have a cold, too?" Agnes asked.

"No. I'm fine. You don't need to worry about me. It's just nausea."

In a familiar cadence, Agnes said, "Caring is careful."

The quote itched at Sarah until she remembered that was something the midwife said. "You've been spending time with Harmony Brite?"

"Sometimes."

Sarah tried again. "I'm really fine. You should catch up with Carmel or someone."

"I don't like being up front."

"You'll just be cold and bored back here."

"Up there, I feel like I'm wearing an itchy sweater made of eyes," Agnes said. "Everyone watches who walks with who."

They did, which meant people would be noticing that Sarah wasn't with Faith, Dorcas, and Mary. Well, no one would blame them for wanting to get rid of her.

Her ears played a mean trick on her and she could almost hear her sister-wives hooting about Toby somewhere in the distance, in the rain.

Sarah gave up and let herself fall into step with her cousin. "Okay, if you want to walk with me, but I'm not in a good mood."

UBI DAY: MORNING

Hannah

The blizzard in New York claimed five lives in a traffic accident outside of Utica. A passenger from the second vehicle, the only one who survived, sat blankly in the back of the traffic officer's car where he'd been sent to get out of the snow. His mom had enjoyed driving in bad weather; she liked challenges. The traffic officer offered him her coffee. It was bitter. That was good.

Thirty miles away in Canastota, Hannah hurried into the street, darting quick, worried glances in every direction even though she could hardly see through the snow. She wondered if everyone could tell she was being paranoid, or whether she just felt like a blazing neon sign.

Ice melt slipped through a tear in her glove. She wrung her hand, feeling the numbness start to settle in. It was almost impossible to believe there had been so many heat deaths here last summer. Underneath layers of down and flannel, she still felt cold and exposed. The constant, nervous itch of being watched ran from her nape down to the small of her back even though she hadn't actually found anyone watching her yet today, unless she counted herself.

Inside, the post office's overworked heater gave off a weird burning smell as it wheezed over the dozen or so people waiting for their turns at the counter. Everyone was swaddled in heavy coats, standing silently or chatting in hushed voices, tapping their toes every once in a while to keep the blood flowing as they thumbed at their phones. A rude teenager slumped in the corner, backpack dangling off of one shoulder as she mouthed silently at a projection on her wrister.

A scratch started up in Hannah's throat—her mold allergies went wild in these old Victorian buildings. She staved off a cough by clearing her throat; the sound echoed between the empty walls and high ceilings, drawing a few inquiring glances before the hush fell again. The weather outside was that kind of smothering snow that left everything quieter.

"Well, look at you, Hannah, joining us early birds," someone said loudly.

Hannah's heart pounded. Abigail? But when she turned toward the voice, she saw the speaker was her landlady, Elizabeth.

The older woman unbuttoned her robin-red coat, revealing one of her usual bulky sweatshirts underneath. This one had a picture of a standoff between Bugs Bunny and Yosemite Sam who were wielding guns that read "eight shooter" and "nine shooter." Her foundation was applied a little too thickly, as was the mascara on her bottom lashes, which had left specks of black on her cheeks. In her ears, she wore the same pair of gold cross studs she'd had on every time Hannah had met her.

"I see you couldn't wait to collect your basic income either," Elizabeth said. "Most of my friends get it by mail, but I believe in doing things myself. If something goes kablooey anyway, you know whose fault it is. What about you?"

Hannah didn't like Elizabeth. She was one of those gossips who wanted to be the center of everything. The clutch of women she belonged to seemed to think that Hannah being new in town gave them the right to pry into whatever they wanted. It was like they expected her to testify. *I was born in St. Louis on a Tuesday in February, and I think lobster is overrated, and I didn't finish my civil engineering degree, and I always pick up my basic income as soon as I can because my ex-wife is a stalker and I only got away from her in the first place because I could finally get enough money to get out on my own. And I take my money as soon as I can every year so I have it on hand for when Abigail gets high and tracks us like a bloodhound—which she does every January fifteenth because that's the anniversary of when we left her. And no, I don't want to talk about it because it's an open wound in my gut, and why can't anyone just respect other people's privacy sometimes, just one damn time?*

"Rent's due," Hannah said shortly.

Her irritation must have come through. Elizabeth looked affronted.

Elizabeth said, "Well, I know *that*."

"Sorry," Hannah said quickly. The last thing she needed was to antagonize her landlady. She tried to force a smile, but she knew it didn't look right. "The cold gets to me."

Elizabeth nodded, but her brows were still raised. "It hits a lot of people that way from time to time." After a beat, she leaned in toward Hannah and tapped her elbow. "How's the house working for you? Not too small?"

Elizabeth had asked before.

"It's fine," Hannah said.

"I guess your two boys are still little enough to be snug as bugs in bunk beds. You'll miss this age," Elizabeth said.

"They do okay," Hannah said.

"There's not much room to play, though," said Elizabeth. "You can always come over with the kids, you know, as long as we have the lights on. We're just a few blocks over. You can leave them for a few hours if you've got errands sometime. Just let us know a bit beforehand. It's only me and Wayne in the house now. There's nothing but space."

Elizabeth had offered before, more than once.

"Sure," Hannah mumbled.

"Just let us know a bit before you come over," Elizabeth said, trying to catch her eye.

"Sure," Hannah repeated, evading her gaze. "We appreciate the offer. We just don't have much time."

"Well, *that's* because you don't ever get someone else to sit for them," Elizabeth pushed. "Unless you've got one of the girls from the high school coming?"

"No, just me."

"You have to get out and do something once in a while. Get into the air. Get your legs in motion. Do you like to hike?"

Hannah made a noncommittal noise.

"Of course, once the weather gets better, you'll have lots of options. Even if you don't like hiking, there's fishing. But just because it's winter now doesn't mean you have to stay shut in. There's an ice rink in the mall if you think the lake's not safe for your boys."

Elizabeth paused, but Hannah stared indistinctly at the floor, pretending not to realize Elizabeth wanted a reaction. She tried not to hunch in on herself protectively.

Elizabeth went on, "What *do* you like to do? Tell me. I can help find you something here. Are you from a city? We don't have a big theater, but they play old movies in the church basement. I'm lending them my Betty Boop tapes this February. It's a popular place for people to take their dates. Every year or two, it seems like some couple who had their first date there is getting married. Are you seeing anyone? There are people around here on their third marriages, even fourth or fifth. No one judges people about it anymore the way they did when I was little. The movies are every other Saturday and last week was off, so there's one coming up. I know you haven't settled in a new church yet, but I think God would be happy to see you in any of His houses, if you know what I mean."

Hannah didn't notice that Elizabeth had stopped talking until she realized she could breathe again. The heater was still wheezing. Someone started arguing with a clerk who said new postal bank accounts couldn't be opened until the teller came in. A few more people had come in from the cold, snow melting on the shoulders of their coats.

"Oh, um, we're Jewish," Hannah said.

Elizabeth looked disappointed, and then rallied. "Well, anyone can come to Saturday movie nights. It's good people."

"Thank you," Hannah said vaguely. "I'll make sure to think about it."

Across the room, a clerk called the next number to be served.

Elizabeth caught back whatever she'd been about to say and pulled out her phone to double-check her service number. "Yep, that's me. Time to show my papers so I can get back a little of what the government steals from us in taxes." Elizabeth paused, and then added in a quieter voice, "I'm glad we don't get crazy protestors up here, don't get me wrong. But sometimes I see the number on my tax forms and I'm about ready to riot, too."

Elizabeth patted Hannah on the arm.

"You get warm," Elizabeth said. "Try standing by the wall over there. Sometimes it's a little better by the vents."

Janelle

In Chicago, traffic was a nightmare. The dismal weather was more than enough to keep everything at a standstill, even with people staying home to avoid the cold over the holiday. Cars crowded the lanes, unmoving, honking discordantly.

Janelle walked into their apartment, threw her purse on the kitchen counter, turned to her sister, and demanded, "All right. Let's see it."

Nevaeh shrank under her sister's glare. Self-consciously, she started shrugging off her coat. Once she had it off of her shoulders, she weaseled behind one of the chairs to try to block her chest as she finished removing the coat in a single maneuver.

Janelle angled her head so she could read Nevaeh's tank top anyway:

FUCK UBI.

REPARATIONS!!

"In all caps, with two exclamation points, no less." Janelle shook her head. "At least you didn't write 'oobi.'"

"I don't know why you hate calling it oobi so much—"

"Because no one says 'fuh-bye' instead of FBI or 'sigh-ay' instead of CIA. And because it sounds stupid." Janelle made a twirling motion with her fingers. "And the back?"

Nevaeh ducked her head.

"Come on," Janelle said.

Nevaeh reluctantly turned around.

"'Forty fucking acres and a fucking mule.' I see college prep vocab is really paying off."

Nevaeh pulled out the chair and sat with her arms crossed. "True. I bet most Americans don't know what an 'acre' is."

"Do *you*?"

"It's a vegetable they fry in the South, right?" Nevaeh rolled her eyes. "It's about forty-eight hundred square yards."

Janelle blinked, mildly surprised. "Huh."

"I looked it up when I made the shirt." Nevaeh made a face as she realized she'd said more than she meant to. "Uh, I did the design."

"I figured it wasn't professional. *Two exclamation points,*" grumbled Janelle. "How many of these did you give out? How many did you make?"

"I don't know. Twenty. There are a couple left in my backpack."

"And because you chose *today* to launch your clothing line, your school was able to make me come in and pick you up immediately because technically it's a holiday and school care is a courtesy."

"I didn't know they'd do that," Nevaeh said, looking embarrassed.

"Nevaeh." Janelle sat down across from her sister. Her tone turned earnest. "You have to take this seriously. I burned a lot of bridges in the old days. Almost all the American-owned aggregators have me on their blacklists. I've been okay working through the Indians and Brazilians because they didn't used to care what their reporters thought about domestic American stuff, but things are changing. A guy ended up on the Brazilian blacklist last month for bad-mouthing President Wells. The Brazilians don't even *like* Wells." She rapped the table in frustration. "We talked about this months ago. You *agreed* to be careful."

"I said I wouldn't go to any political *events*," Nevaeh mumbled.

"Come on, Nevaeh, you're too old to pretend you didn't know the context when I said no 'political activity.'"

"How was I supposed to know wearing a shirt would count?"

Janelle shook her head. "'Fuck UBI. Forty fucking acres and a fucking mule.' I think 'most Americans' know that's political activity. What do you expect me to do if you're going to act like this? You have to pull it now when I'm trying to earn a fifth of our yearly income? You don't like rent and food?"

At some point, Nevaeh had uncrossed her arms and worked up her self-righteousness. "I don't *like* that giving handouts to everyone won't solve the economic gap caused by slavery."

"It's making it better."

"Not enough."

Janelle shrugged. "What's enough?"

Nevaeh leaned over the table. "I know you don't really think like this!"

Janelle stared back at her for a flat second. "Kids never understand history." She walked over to the counter to fuss with her purse so she'd have something to do with her hands. "You don't know how different it is that so many people in your high school class can go to college."

"I read all your old UBI articles," Nevaeh said.

"Some of those kids would have had to drop out before they even graduated from high school to help support their families."

"I searched your old pen name in the house files," Nevaeh said.

"Some of them might have been murdered by police." Janelle stopped, registering what Nevaeh had just said. "Wait, you did what?"

Nevaeh raised her hands defensively. "None of it was locked! I didn't look at anything *private*." She added, "I don't believe you've really changed everything you think."

"What I *think*—and what I *thought*—is that UBI is better than having nothing."

Nevaeh started to respond. Janelle held up her hand.

Janelle continued, "What I *think*—and what I *thought*—is that we had an extraordinary moment of political will after Winter Night. The whole country was breathing a sigh of relief. We weren't just trying to get ourselves back on track; we were trying to figure out what kind of track to get on. It was like we had this dream together of improving the world."

"Right! So—"

"What I *said* was that it would be a one-shot deal. We had one sure arrow to fire from that bow. And whatever we didn't make sure to fix then, it probably wasn't going to get fixed for a long time."

"You were right!"

"Yeah. I was." Janelle toyed with the zipper on her purse. "UBI is definitely better than having nothing."

"But you were right about *everything*," Nevaeh said. "You called it patchwork legislation."

"It is."

"You said once the opposition realized UBI was definitely happening, they were going to try to make it hard to collect. Like drumming up paranoia about bank breaches to make us use checks and the mail. You said they'd start saying states needed the right to make their own rules, but they'd really mean states should be able to make people jump through hoops. You said it was 'enshrining unequal access.'"

Janelle shrugged. "And now the law's been written."

"We can write it again!"

"Good. Good luck," said Janelle. "In the meantime, I have to take care of you, and not lose our source of income. Can I trust you to do what you say you'll do? Or are you going to play more word games?"

"I'm fine. Go do your interviews."

Janelle zipped up her purse, picked it up, and then made a decision. "Good. You can come with me."

"Why?"

"Because I cannot think of *anything* more annoying than having to go through my day today."

"Fine," grumbled Nevaeh.

"For the rest of your punishment—"

Nevaeh made a face. "Having to go with you isn't enough?"

"For the rest of your punishment," said Janelle, "serious or silly? Your pick."

"What's the serious punishment?" Nevaeh asked.

"Stay in for the week. No windfall parties."

"Bleh. What's the silly one?"

Janelle took an ominous pause. *"The ugly shirt."*

Neveah wrinkled her nose. "Oh yuck, really?"

"From when we leave until we get home."

Nevaeh considered. ". . . Then I can go to Deja's party on Friday?"

"Sure, as long as you wear the ugly shirt there, too."

"Come on!"

"Just kidding."

"Fine. I'll take the ugly shirt."

Janelle pointed to the hallway. "It's in my closet."

Nevaeh made a show of slouching into the hallway for dramatic effect.

Janelle had found the ugly shirt while she was cleaning out their parents' closet after the plane crash. Someone had apparently given it to their mother as a gag gift. Its worst feature was the huge pearl buttons that someone had drawn smileys on with black marker. They looked like the kind of haunted faces that emerge from the walls in horror movies. Janelle had felt a strange obligation not to throw it away because, in its own awful way, it had achieved perfection.

A few minutes later, Nevaeh returned, drowning in the mess of polka dots and ruffles.

"I don't know how, but I swear it's getting uglier," Nevaeh complained.

"How much do you want to get rid of it?" Janelle asked. "I'm sure we could find something else. You had this cute little pumpkin costume when you were a baby. Do you think we could find one for teens?"

"Feh."

"Come on. I need to get as much on camera as I can, and then get back here to call a friend of mine tonight. I'm *really* behind."

Olivia

In Colorado, the sun had emerged to scatter the snow with glitter. The day was outrageously bright and perfect. The glistening slopes looked so soft; it seemed like rolling around on them would be like rolling on feathers. They looked delicious, too: enormous snow cones, flavored with sunlight.

Olivia smiled at the mountains through the window as the strangers William had brought with him jostled into the room.

"About time, asshole!" shouted Leroy.

Olivia turned to look. Leroy had raised his hands to his mouth like a megaphone, which wasn't really necessary, but it showed off his arms, which was the kind of thing Leroy liked to do. That was why his T-shirt from Yale swimming was a size too small. His headband was trendy, but unlike a lot of guys, he actually needed it to keep his hair from falling into his eyes.

William jumped up onto the piano bench. "Indeed! Time waits for none of us, including me."

He clapped his hands together to call everyone's

attention.

"Sisters, Misters, and Twisters! Tune in your wristers!" William raised his arms and pointed to his Rolex wrister. It looked like oystersteel and gold with diamonds and a green sapphire face.

The room kept getting louder as more people giggled and shuffled their way in.

"Jesus, how many people did he invite?" asked Katie. "It looks like . . . thirty?"

It was hard to count through the alcohol. Olivia scanned the room quickly. "Yeah, maybe twenty-eight."

Katie mouthed to herself for a few seconds as she looked around. "You're right. Twenty-eight."

A guy sat down heavily next to Olivia where there wasn't enough room, pushing her toward the other side of the couch. He could have sat down just fine next to Katie, but people did this kind of thing a lot. They'd look at Olivia and just decide there was room. People didn't do it as often to Katie because she was bony, but tall. Olivia was just small all around.

Before Katie could scoot to make more space, someone else had already taken a seat on her other side.

A random person exclaimed, "There's a fucking grand piano in here!"

People laughed for different reasons.

William laughed loudest. "That's right! There's a piano! And not one, but two chandeliers! Behold the rustic charm of Versailles!" He waved his arms back and forth. "Tune in your wristers!"

Some girl perched on the lap of the guy sitting next to Olivia. She flashed Olivia a scornful look.

Olivia ignored her as she lifted her hand. She loved her wrister more than anything else she owned. It was rare and pretty, and it made her seem more interesting than she was.

She'd spent her entire disbursement on it last year. She'd taken weeks carefully choosing each detail. It was a Tiffany piece with a slender, tasteful rose-gold band. The fixture was shaped like a butterfly with delicately engraved wings. Olivia liked to run her fingers over the wings sometimes to feel the etched patterns.

The wrister made her feel like an adult, finally free of the enameled ballet ribbons that her mom had given her on her tenth birthday and wanted her to wear forever. Even though she was eighteen, Olivia's mom had tried to stop Olivia from switching to a new wrister until her dad had put his foot down.

She folded back the butterfly wings to open the projector. A note from the family accountant flashed on her contacts. She saw some words as she blinked it away. Her oobi deposit had been sent into the security maze. It would be ready in her vault account in a few hours.

She switched the projection view from flat to tall. A fizz of sky blue appeared, about the size of a clutch purse. The fizz resolved into a weird, swooping image.

"Stop swinging your arms around!" someone shouted at William. "You're going to make me throw up."

Many people called out their agreement. Olivia realized that William was wavving everyone the view from his wrister. He stopped swinging his wrist, and angled it to show his face instead.

"What are you making me look at you for?" shouted Leroy in his only-sort-of-joking voice. "I already see too much of your ugly snout!"

"Whoop! Whoop!" Pauline shouted, cutting Leroy off before he could keep sniping. *"Waste Day!"*

"Thank you, Pauline!" William called, sounding like an award show host who was annoyed with his audience. "As my friend is so ably demonstrating with her shot of Don Julio Real—"

"Tres Cuatro Cinco, actually!" Pauline raised the empty shot glass.

William went on, "—of Tres Cuatro Cinco, our glorious Waste Day tradition has always involved the kind of Bacchanalian revelry our ancestors the Greeks"—he paused to indicate a digression—"both the ancients and our late, lamented Greek system—"

People cheered.

He shouted, "—the Bacchanalian revelry our ancestors the Greeks could only wish for! We have imbibed the fruits of the grape, of agave, sugarcane, and barley. We've smoked up and cocked up and coked up and shot up. Danced with our heroines! Our dusty Angels! Our Mary Janes! Our ecstatic Mollies! When we're all burning with Angie's bones in the hellfire, what will be left? The roaches and the snow!"

The room roared with laughter, whooping, and some groans.

William clicked the heels of his oxfords. "We've come, come, come to the orgies! We've bumped our bumps. We've dicked with our dicks. We've feasted on the bean and the taco, tickled the pickle and plums. We've lapped and licked, we cunning linguists! The best death is the little one!"

There was even more cheering. Some people shouted out offers to do one thing or another.

"Now, as Dionysus and Eros await their annual dues, I offer you a different entertainment!"

Katie muttered, "Jesus Christ, I guess he really liked freshman history."

Olivia glanced at the people around them. They were all strangers, so she felt okay saying, "William always talked like that."

Katie balked, affronted, then tugged anxiously on her

ponytail. "I guess . . ." She made a small noise of realization. "I guess you're right. It used to seem so—"

"Your attention, please!" William shouted loudly enough to cut through people's chatter.

"—profound," finished Katie.

A butch-looking college girl popped into the projection. Short canary-yellow hair bristled over her ears. She wore an amazing zippery red leather jacket that looked Italian. Her jeans were that metallic charred gold that had gotten so popular last spring that there was a backlash. Now no one would wear it, which was too bad because Olivia had a dress in it she liked. The butch-looking girl wasn't wearing a wrister at all, which was weird, but not too weird, since it was probably just for the wavve.

The college girl was in a loop. She started out with a wink, her hands tucked behind her back. She did a jump-step and swung out her right arm to show off a bottle of wine. She stuck out her tongue, waved the bottle around, and restarted.

William said, "My friends, in one hour, everyone's favorite U/Me hosts, Chappy and Caesar, are going to announce this year's Waste Day contest. In sixty minutes, fans all over this country are going to find out this year's challenge. However! *We* don't have to wait. If you're lucky enough to be in this room, you can hear it *right now*. In their infinite munificence, C&C have chosen a few devoted fans to get access to this morning's show in advance. I'm one of the lucky bastards who's been favored by fate, and now so are you. This is my Waste Day gift to you." He paused for effect. "A head start!"

"So what's the contest?" someone shouted from the kitchenette.

"Getting to it, getting to it," said William.

People groaned. William ignored them.

William went on, "Last year, we competed to see who could find the funniest way to trash our money without spending it."

"I won by shoving it up my ass!" shouted a guy in the audience, laughing. Other people shushed him.

"Is it still there?" asked William.

The laughter veered toward his side.

William continued, "Our extremely creative friend here has accidentally illustrated my point! Did he win last year? Is he N. Waters, self-made businessman from Nebraska who used dollar bills to make an enormous papier-mâché sculpture of his own dick? We all know the answer! He is not. But he wants to be a winner so much that he lies even when it's obvious he'll get caught." William waved his hand. "No, don't boo him—he's just like all of us!"

William raised his arms grandly.

He went on, "The year before last, when we used our disbursements to see who could send the most disgusting thing to Congress, who won then? Who paid hundreds of college girls to make personalized bouquets with their used tampons? Do you know who? Anyone? I'll tell you. Not any of us!"

A knot of people had clustered around William, shouting and laughing in all the right places. Katie's eyes were glazed. She mumbled inaudibly to herself. Olivia touched her arm to see if she was okay, but Katie shrugged her off.

William continued, "When C&C kicked things off lo those many years ago, back in the days of our innocence when we competed to maximize the impact of our donations to charity, did any of us snatch the title of best philanthropist? Does all that potable water in Africa run to taps *we* distributed?"

"No!" returned a dozen shouts.

William popped the collar of his vintage jacket. "Well, *amicis,* I don't know about you, but I'm sick of losing. Let's make this year different! Here's C&C!"

The butch college girl's projection moved into a new loop. She shoved the bottle in front of her to show off the label.

Caesar's rumbly voice broadcast through William's U/Me. "This year's much-anticipated contest is in honor of Eve Lawrence of Ithaca, New York! While we've been jockeying around with trash and charity and all that other great shit, Eve sprayed her scent on the essential Waste Day challenge."

Chappy squeaked, "Let 'er rip!"

The projection of Eve swung the bottle behind her back again. She said, "Our nation keeps pouring money into Basic Income bullshit. So I poured my disbursement into a bottle of Montrachet so I could—"

The angle of the projection was suddenly wider, and the image jumped forward in time. Eve stood with one leg on the seat of her motorcycle, pants and underwear pulled down.

Her voice continued the narration. "—piss it away!"

Eve adjusted the angle of her pelvis. A yellow arc suddenly sprayed straight at Olivia. She flinched.

The room burst out in exclamations.

"What the fuck?" said the guy next to Olivia.

"Gross!" said the girl on his lap.

"Oh my God! Why didn't you warn us?" shouted Elsa from across the room.

Chappy and Caesar were throwing out puns.

"The girl's worth her weight in golden showers!"

"Everything's better with a squeeze of lemon!"

"Is it just me or are you a weeeee bit horny?"

"Think she wants to see my pee pee?"

The loop changed again to show Eve doing tricks on her motorcycle.

Caesar said, "This year, it's all in the name. It's Waste Day! So waste that cash someone else worked hard to earn! Be clever. Be creative. Don't just send your money down the shitter."

"Or do!" squeaked Chappy.

"This year for Waste Day," said Caesar, "waste!"

Eve disappeared. William's face popped back onto the projections that hadn't been shut off in disgust.

"We've got the bread," shouted William. "Off to the circuses!"

Don called, "What's the prize?"

William scanned the room to look straight at him. "Who cares?"

Sarah

The Utah rain was indecisive, alternating between a stinging drizzle and an omnipresent haze. For a few brief minutes, the clouds screwed up their courage and rained like they were trying to wash the sky away, but they were soon exhausted, and resumed their rhythm.

Sarah and Agnes kept going along the long, dreary stretch of road. Apart from the occasional muddy crossroad stretching toward something distantly lost in the rain, nothing changed but the signs.

Agnes picked nervously at the skin on her arms. "Why aren't you in a good mood?"

"Because I'm not," Sarah said flatly.

"Because something's wrong?"

"Because I'm not in a good mood."

"Do you not want to talk about it?"

"Correct."

They walked in silence awhile, through the smells of wet asphalt and wet soil.

At the end of one of the dirt crossroads, a long-gone truck had gouged a course of huge mud puddles. Agnes made a few quick jumps to the other side. Sarah lifted her skirt and picked her way through. As if the slippery ground weren't bad enough, her balance was also thrown off by her nausea and the size of her belly.

Waiting, Agnes chewed her cuticles. Suddenly, she burst out, "Are you in a bad mood because of the baby?"

Taken by surprise, Sarah didn't have time to stop her angry stare.

Agnes jumped back a little. "Sorry. I forgot you didn't want to talk. Sorry."

Sarah cleared her face. "It's not the baby."

"Oh. Good." Agnes didn't sound convinced.

Sarah reached the other side and they went on.

The weather began to lighten, a few streaks of pale sunlight striping the road, but the ground was still muddy and uneven. A cleaner, open smell mixed with the mustiness of the rain. Through the clearer air, they could see pastel clusters of women and children far ahead, made slightly indistinct by patches of light rain.

There were patterns to how people walked year after year. It was almost like a migration. Any one person might be in a different place, but the formation stayed the same. Back here, by now, there would be empty stretches between the lagging groups. Up front, the groups would be clustered together.

A few cars passed in a row, whipping wind in their direction. Someone leaned out of a pickup's passenger window to shout at them.

Suddenly, the image flashed, that terrible memory: Toby's face shoved against the window of their father's truck, nose squashed, the cut on his forehead leaving smears of red. Toby's palms smacking the window on either side of his face, positioned to leave perfect, dirty handprints. His lips making weird shapes against the glass as he shouted. He'd been looking for help. Had he been waiting for her? Had he known she was there?

Her heart slammed as her nausea surged. Bile burned her throat. She doubled over. She almost screamed for him. *Almost.*

By the time she had her breath back, the real truck was gone. Tears rushed hotly into Sarah's eyes, and suddenly she was furious. Her hands knotted up. She wanted to punch something—her fist into her palm if nothing else, just something—but if she started, she didn't know if she'd stop again, or if she'd end up crouched on the side of the road, punching the mud and shouting and sobbing and giving everyone more things to gossip about.

Agnes asked nervously, "Is it still the baby? Sorry I'm asking. Sorry."

Wonderful, now she was scaring Agnes, but she didn't know how to stop. It was all she had to straighten up and get moving again.

"Yeah," Sarah said. "Sure."

Agnes cleared her throat. "I, uh—I'm glad you and the baby are safe, though."

Agnes cowered as she glanced at Sarah to see what she'd do. Sarah didn't say anything.

"I mean—" Agnes said, still looking wary. "It's okay to talk about what *isn't* wrong, right?" Agnes paused another half second, biting her lip as she watched Sarah's face. When Sarah still didn't object, Agnes continued in a teacher-like tone. "A lot of women say the first one is hardest because you don't know what's going to happen, but then other women say it's easiest because you're young and your body doesn't have as much trouble going back to normal. I said to Mrs. Brite it looks to me like both are right to me in different ways, and she said she thought so, too."

"Why are you spending so much time with Mrs. Brite?"

"I go with her when the babies are being born."

"Why?"

"I helped with a baby cow at the Walthers'. It was stuck and I had the smallest hands." Agnes held up her hands proudly. "Mrs. Brite said these days we need more help with women than cows and I could go around with her. Did you know the Walthers have things on their barns that burn up the cow farts? They get electricity off of it."

"You helped at the Walthers'? That calf came *early*," said Sarah.

"No, it was a *late* calf," Agnes corrected. "It happened last March."

Sarah frowned. "You've been doing this for a year, and I didn't know?"

"Almost a year," Agnes said with a hint of resentment. "Three out of four parts of a year."

Sarah shook her head, frowning as she thought back. She remembered telling Agnes "not now" a few times when she tried to come talk, but had it really been almost a year?

A year ago. That was around the time when her mother died. Around when they'd told Sarah she was getting married. Around when her father had married Trinity and put the baby in her that was four weeks old now.

If she didn't concentrate, her memories of all the things that had happened during the last year blurred together like smudges of chalk melting into the sidewalk. Months seemed to merge into a single exhausted, unquiet night. Sometimes the voices she remembered filtering under her bedroom door were her sister-wives', and sometimes they were her sisters'. Sometimes she remembered being in the converted closet at her husband's house; sometimes she remembered the big shared room at her father's. Mostly, she remembered the claustrophobia of staring for hours at the static behind her eyelids, trapped awake.

Then suddenly, it was like someone had shone a painfully bright flashlight into her eyes—and the flashlight was the headlights of her father's truck as the engine rattled awake. The pickup sat there, grinding and stinking, the whole time Dad and her brothers beat Toby up. She'd started out standing behind the truck bed, but she must have done something she didn't remember, because then she was sprawled on the ground in front of the truck with a cut on her arm. She tried to get up, but the baby kept her down. If she'd managed to stand, they'd just have moved her anyway, carried her back to her husband's house for her sister-wives to peck at. On the ground, she was a witness, watching Toby's face pressed against the window until the flare of the headlights swallowed everything up.

"Sarah," Agnes ventured.

Sarah shifted back to the present. Toby wasn't here; Agnes was. Sarah swept a hair out of her face to give herself a second to recover. "I didn't know it had been so long since we talked last."

"You didn't want to talk," Agnes said tightly.

"I didn't realize."

"*I* realized."

Glancing over, Sarah saw that Agnes's face was

bunched up as if she were trying not to cry. Her eyes had pinked, and her chest shook with the effort of keeping silent.

Embarrassed at seeing something Agnes probably hadn't wanted her to, Sarah looked away again quickly. "Sorry."

Agnes said, "I don't know anyone you still talk to. Why don't you talk to anyone? Is it because you're married? I thought it was, but a lot of girls get married and don't do that."

"I talk to Faith, Dorcas, and Mary." Sarah's laugh came out more bitterly than she'd intended.

"Why is that funny?" asked Agnes, looking worried she'd missed something.

"It's not." Well, it shouldn't have been. "I just get tired lately."

Agnes nodded. "Because of the baby."

"Sure."

There was a dead furry thing on an intersecting road. It looked like it might have been a cat. Sarah moved Agnes so she wouldn't see it.

Slowly, Sarah asked, "Agnes, do you remember Clement?"

Immediately, Sarah regretted bringing it up.

Agnes made a face, thinking. Sarah tried to ignore the memory of Toby's face in the truck.

"Yeah," Agnes said. She gave a sudden, snorting laugh as if she'd surprised herself. "He, you know, a lot. Farted."

Sarah nodded, trying to pretend asking had just been a stray thought.

"You don't see Clement around anymore." Agnes paused. "Because he had to go."

Agnes paused again and looked at Sarah. Agnes was too smart. When things didn't fit, she worried at them like a teething puppy.

Agnes ventured, "He was inappropriate with the prophet's wives."

Sarah choked back a surge of anger. All those excuses. All those boys. All those lies like barbed hooks stuck everywhere.

Dubiously, Agnes asked, "You're still just feeling sick with the baby?"

Sarah focused on her feet. "Yes."

"Sarah . . ."

They passed into a strip of rain that plished and ploshed around them. Sarah hunched and lowered her head as if she were pushing against a huge wind.

"Sarah?" Agnes tried again. "Um, Sarah?"

"What?"

"Um . . . why isn't Toby here?"

"What do you mean?"

"Because I saw your other brothers and sisters and

their moms, but I didn't see Toby."

"Maybe you missed him."

"But why isn't he with them?"

Sarah sped up. Her patience was stretched like a rubber band. "Because he's not."

"Because he's usually at our youth study, but he hasn't been." Agnes's shoes splashed mud as she skipped to keep up.

"Stop," Sarah said. "I don't want to talk about this."

"Because he really likes youth study."

"Don't be a busybody."

"He doesn't miss it hardly ever."

"Stop."

"He even tries to go when he's sick. Sarah... I heard some things... Sarah? Because I heard it's like Clement... Sarah?... I heard—"

Sarah cut off walking mid-step. She rebalanced and turned on Agnes in one move. "Stop it! Stop! Agnes, will you ever stop talking!"

Agnes shrank like a turtle.

"You talk too much," Sarah spilled. "That's why people don't want you around. You need to learn when people want you to back off. You need to listen when someone tells you to stop! You want to know what happened to Toby?"

She leaned over her cousin, hands raised and spread

wide, not thinking about how it made her look bigger. Still cringing, Agnes nodded.

"He got driven off to the side of the highway and left there. Without food, without money, without anything. They bloodied him up and they dumped him. It's what happened to Clement. It's what happened to Bartholomew. It's going to happen again to someone else and he'll just disappear and his family won't even talk about him." Sarah's voice was raw. "He'll just be gone. Toby's gone."

"That's not what happens," Agnes said in a small voice.

"It happens. Dorcas throwing red into my white laundry so I'll get yelled at when it's pink? It happens. Mary hiding my garment while I shower? Faith telling everyone so often that she's worried I'll flirt with boys that people have forgotten I never actually did it? It happens. Toby getting driven off with blood in his eye? It happens! Maybe you'd better get used to it before you need Mrs. Brite yourself. Ask *her* what happens. I'm sure she knows."

Sarah ran out of breath.

Agnes whispered, "Keep sweet."

Her eyes were round and scared like Toby's had been.

Sarah looked around to make sure no one had heard, but they were far behind almost everyone now.

Sarah didn't keep sweet. That was her problem. She'd always been too angry. She said no. She didn't smile.

Toby was gentle, but the wrong way for a boy. He always let everyone else choose first. He was weak and he cried too easily.

Agnes was too smart, too needy, too scared.

They were all bent nails trying to keep their lives tacked together. No wonder everything kept coming apart.

"We shouldn't talk about him," Sarah said almost under her breath. "He's gone."

UBI DAY: MIDDAY

Hannah

In Canastota, the storm showed some leniency. Snow veiled the world in white instead of obliterating it. The wind seemed resentful at being left alone, batting angrily at the trees as it swept the streets.

The air in the post office smelled stale from all the people still standing in line. Hannah folded her disbursement check into her pocket as she turned away from the service counter. She rubbed the paper between her thumb and forefinger to remind herself it was really there.

Now that she had her check, she could get back to the boys and stay inside with them for the next few days while Abigail would be searching hardest. Hannah wouldn't have to leave her two fragile, tenderhearted little children alone to keep the wolf away from their door by themselves—at least, not until the next emergency.

Letting go of the check long enough to tug on her gloves, she wiped her eyes with the back of her hand. Sometimes, she worried the only way this would stop was if Abigail got them back or somebody died. Hannah didn't want to keep running, but running was better than either of those.

As Hannah moved toward the door, Elizabeth walked over from where she'd been lingering by the sorting machines. She was in the process of buttoning her coat collar, but it was clear she'd been ready to go for a while.

"As long as you're here, I'll head back to the house with you. You can write me a check." Elizabeth added, in a joking cadence but with a prickly tone, "As you said, rent's due."

Hannah balked. "I don't want you to go out of your way. I'll drop it in your mailbox tomorrow."

"Nah, this way no one has to face this storm more than once. I'm sure you'd rather be in with those boys tomorrow, not trudging through the snow."

"I don't know," Hannah said, stalling. She grabbed the first idea she could think of. "Aren't you worried about falling?"

Elizabeth's eyebrows raised in indignation. "Why? Do I look frail to you?"

"No—"

"Old's not the same as useless, you know." Elizabeth shook her head. Her face was slightly red. "Dear, don't worry about me. Young people die from falling too, you know, but they think they're invincible, so they aren't careful until they get older. If they manage to get older.

You ask a safety officer sometime when they're not doing much. They'll tell you about the girl who came out visiting from away in Texas and cracked her head open on the curb in front of the bank."

Hannah swallowed. She could think of one or two more things to try that might get Elizabeth to back off, but she was worried about getting to the point where protesting more would make her look hostile and suspicious. She gave a vague, resigned nod instead.

She spent several minutes fussing with her coat and hat in case Elizabeth would get frustrated and leave, but she didn't. They headed out into the snow together. Everything around them was filtered through white, but at least they could see.

The wind stung Hannah's cheeks as she restlessly scanned their environment, searching for signs of someone hiding among the trees or crouched behind a parked car. A few cars passed slowly, their shapes showing darkly through the snow like metal behemoths plodding past.

Snow made things directionless. Someone's cat was on their porch, meowing to get in. There was the sound of a door. It could have come from any of the nearby houses.

Elizabeth asked, "So, your boys, what happened to their father?"

Hannah swallowed her bitter response: *Actually, she*

still comes by to beat me up sometimes, and said tightly, "We left."

"You left him? Oh, what a pity."

Oh, what a pity. The phrase cut straight through Hannah's gut. What a *pity.* Her hands, concealed in their coat pockets, bunched into fists of their own accord.

She snapped, "*Her.*"

"Her," Elizabeth repeated crisply.

Thankfully, they couldn't talk much more on the walk home; the wind picked up until hearing was almost impossible. For the last two blocks, they had to walk straight into it. It battered at them, trying to shove them backward.

Hannah counted the blurred black shapes of mailboxes until they reached hers. Someone, probably Elizabeth, had painted a cartoon on the side of the mailbox long enough ago that the paint was wearing, but not so long ago that it had faded into incomprehensibility. It showed Snoopy standing guard on top of his doghouse. The drawing was pretty good for an amateur's except that Snoopy's expression came across as disappointed instead of watchful. Close up, it seemed like he was staring morosely at the snow.

The mailbox flag was down. Hannah felt her breath flow out with relief even though she hadn't realized she was holding it in. Abigail had never attacked them from a distance—not so far—but Hannah still kept thinking about things like seizure cards and mail bombs, and those envelopes full of Anthrax that she'd heard about on a documentary once when she was so little that her parents hadn't thought she'd be able to understand what the voice-over was talking about. It had terrified her for months, the thought that someone could just send death to you with a stamp.

Hannah was close enough to see the weird look Elizabeth was giving her. She gave a quick shrug in return as if she'd just been irritated that the mail carriers hadn't yet forced their way through the cold.

Hannah went up the porch steps first, glancing over her shoulder as often as she could without tripping. The lock on the rental house was always stubborn, but some days were worse than others, especially with cold, gloved hands. She yanked on the door and wrenched the key, but it wouldn't budge.

Elizabeth gave Hannah an irritated look. "Take your time."

Hannah was about fed up. She yanked again, and finally the key turned.

"See? You've just got to relax," Elizabeth said.

Hannah decided to pretend she hadn't heard. She shoved the door open, but before she could rush inside, Elizabeth caught her shoulder.

"I'm the one who has to clean the rugs between tenants," Elizabeth said, diligently wiping her feet. She gestured at the mat.

"I need to get *inside*," said Hannah.

Elizabeth tsked. "We *can* be civilized, *even* in the cold."

Elizabeth's condescending tone made Hannah's blood surge. She was over thirty. She was no one's daughter anymore; her parents were dead. She did not need to be babied and pushed around. She'd had enough of it living with Abigail, who wanted control over every little thing, whether it was how often Hannah filed her fingernails or whether the weird sound the truck was making meant they should take it to the mechanic. She needed to *get inside to the boys,* that was what mattered.

Knowing it would cause problems if she didn't, Hannah bitterly wasted time scraping her shoes anyway.

Finally, the door was closed behind them. Hannah took a second to concentrate on her breath. She pulled off her gloves, kissed her fingertip, and touched the mezuzah in the doorway.

Elizabeth hung her coat on the rack, but Hannah kept hers on. She didn't want to encourage Elizabeth to think she should make herself comfortable.

"I'm home," Hannah called up the stairs to Jake and Isaiah. "Stay where you are."

"Oh, aren't your boys coming down?" Elizabeth asked, disappointed.

"They have homework," Hannah lied.

"Oh, is your littlest in kindergarten already?"

She swapped to a different lie. "Jake has homework. Isaiah likes to 'help' him with it."

"That can wait, can't it?"

Hannah cleared her throat. "Let me get my checkbook."

"Are you sure they can't come down? Just a little while."

Hannah opened the middle drawer of the end table nearest the stairs. "My checkbook's in here. Give me a minute to find it."

"No need to rush on my account. I should probably stay awhile anyway. The weather report says it's going to get better later, and they're right these days, most of the time. You don't want to throw me out in the cold."

Hannah worked to unclench her jaw. This had obviously been Elizabeth's plan all along. As neutrally as she could, she said, "I don't think we can do that today."

Elizabeth's eyebrow raised. "Big plans for your oobi?"

Hannah found the checkbook and shut the drawer. "No—" she said automatically, and then wondered if lying might be more likely to get Elizabeth to leave. "—Yes," she corrected herself. "We have a little Windfall Day family tradition for just the three of us. Sorry, it just won't work."

"Well then, maybe you can br—"

A rumbling came from outside, only barely loud enough to be distinguishable from the general chaos of the storm.

Hannah turned slowly toward the door. She felt like Rugelach, the cat she'd had when she was a kid. It had always known exactly when to come running to the door to greet Hannah's father. It didn't care about any other car engine, just his. It knew that car as well as it knew its own meow.

Every breath in Hannah's body knew this engine. A Lewis compact utility. Blue paint, missing license plate frame, the driver's and passenger's seats upholstered in different leathers. A felt rainbow above the audio console like a multicolored unibrow, and a goatee sticker below the dials. Seventeen years old and running strong because Lewis CUs were really built to last.

Hannah's hands felt cold, and a sick spinning began in her stomach.

Janelle

The trains were swamped with people and weather delays. It only got worse when the rain decided to freeze into hail. For half an hour, the sky spat balls of ice at people scurrying between shelters, until eventually the hail got bored and dissolved into rain again, leaving slippery layers of refrozen slush.

Frankly, the moody and unpleasant weather reflected Janelle's feelings about the day so far.

She led Nevaeh off the train two stops early and told her to brace for misery. Before they could even start off, Janelle's buggy followcam gave a dying shriek loud enough to hear through her purse.

She and Nevaeh bustled into the public restrooms near the station. Steam heating amplified the odor of urine, and made them sweat in the winter coats that would feel way too light once they went back outside.

"It's dead." Janelle prodded it, smacked it, and shook it like a martini. "Motherfu—"

Nevaeh grabbed it out of her hand. "Let me see it."

Janelle let her take it. It rankled that Nevaeh was better

with technology than she was. She still thought of herself as more whiz kid than wizened.

Nevaeh began by tapping the thing around its circumference, and then started doing things like holding it up to her ear and sniffing its speakers. Janelle felt like she was watching a faith healer. She was miffed that she couldn't tell whether or not Nevaeh was pranking her. Her sister shook the thing, turned it half a twist in her hand, and then gave it back.

"Yep, totally broken," she said.

Janelle grumbled. She stared at the useless silver tennis ball and hoped like hell it was still under warranty, because she wasn't sure how she could possibly afford another one.

The aggregators didn't like it when she did interviews with just one camera since it so dramatically cut back the amount of material that could be spliced together, but she didn't have much choice. Janelle resisted the urge to practice her overhand, and stuck the dead buzzcam in her purse.

Aboveground, the icy wind seemed to blow straight through their winter gear. Janelle and Nevaeh trudged in tandem, hunched in their coats to save a bit of warmth, occasionally flicking empathetic looks at one another.

Their first interview: Justine Wythe Elementary and Middle School.

Kindergarten through eighth grade, a clashing population of well-off students (mostly White) and disadvantaged students (White, Black, and Hispanic). Students had a green, navy, and white uniform that was modeled—as these things seemed to be, for unfathomable reasons—after the ones from 1950s Catholic schools with lots of pleats and buttons. Mostly, the pleats were not ironed, and a significant percentage of shirts were buttoned askew.

They sent her to a third-grade class.

"Oh God," Janelle said as she and Nevaeh followed the principal's assistant through several hallways. "Why can't it at least be the twelve-year-olds?"

"Would you like them better in pumpkin costumes?" Nevaeh asked.

"Heh," said Janelle.

"How about in . . . F-UBI shirts?" Nevaeh asked, glancing around to make sure her whispered comments wouldn't be overheard. "Printed on bitty tank tops in rainbow cam?"

Janelle rolled her eyes.

"You know it would be pretty rad," said Nevaeh.

"Do you have to say *rad*?" complained Janelle. "It makes me feel like I'm about to walk into a John Hughes movie and bump into Molly Ringwald."

"Who's Molly Ringwald?"

"Augh. Not again. You literally *require* a Classic Hollywood night," Janelle said. "Old Hollywood! Those eighties dresses! The *glamour*. They used to understand *classic* beauty. Julia Roberts, Rae Dawn Chong, Jennifer Beals, Demi Moore, Lisa Bonet . . ."

"I don't like movies in black and white."

"Black and white? Are you kidding?"

"No?"

"You're decades off, little girl," said Janelle.

"I am?" Nevaeh asked, wide-eyed. "But World War II was in the eighties, right?"

Janelle's breath hitched for a rant, and then she caught a glimpse of Nevaeh's overly serious face. She snorted. "You're *definitely* screwing with me. My own little sister, screwing with me."

The classroom smelled like classroom: paste, kids, construction paper, the distinguished aroma of print books, which is actually the smell of mold. Gently thrashed tablets were attached to roughly thrashed desks at which sat the kids doing the thrashing. School supplies sprawled garishly across every surface: hot-pink packs, bright yellow timers, big fat markers in all colors of the rainbow, neon asthma inhalers, styluses wrapped in holographic paper.

Only about 25 percent of the seats were filled. Presumably, the other families had found a way to take advantage of the holiday.

A small group of sullen-looking twelve-year-olds sat in

a cluster near the wall. Janelle briefly hoped that meant she'd be able to interview them instead of the younger ones, but the teacher only gestured to them as they passed. "Not enough students in their grade came in today. We merged classrooms."

They showed Janelle and Nevaeh to a nook in the back where three students were lined up.

"My best and brightest," the teacher said, looking harried. Pleading for sympathy, they added, "Everyone who came in today is riled up. It's a nightmare. I didn't sign up to do school care. If the program survives review next year, I may quit, I tell you."

The teacher rushed away again. Janelle thumbed on her single remaining buzzcam as she assessed the students.

Their racial diversity mirrored the school's—not surprising; a lot of schools did that for interviews. It looked like they were probably all girls: one wore glittery beaded bands on her braids; one had a sprinkling of costume jewelry; and the last was wearing a stiff, formal white dress that looked like its usual outing was to the ballet, and which was definitely *not* part of the uniform.

Janelle introduced herself, got their names which she promptly forgot (luckily, her buzzcam was still recording), and automatically paused to ask for pronouns. She cut herself off just in time. There were parents who'd get fussy these days about asking for gender, despite every basic rule of courtesy Janelle had grown up with all her life, thank you very much.

Nevaeh jumped into the pause with a grin. "Hey, little folks! I'm she. Y'all she?"

Janelle grimaced. For Christ's sake.

The—apparently all girls—said yes.

"She-beasts! Femme? Femme? Femme? Yesss," Nevaeh declared, proudly going down the line and doing that hand-clasp thing every single person under eighteen seemed to have learned simultaneously last summer.

At least her sister was charming.

Janelle heard someone mumble the word *trendy* and glanced back to see the teacher had returned to lurk a few feet away. Ugh. Whatever, just as long as the teacher left their comments at that. The being-a-girl-is-trendy people could get really nasty to Nevaeh.

"This is my sister, Nevaeh. Doesn't she have a nice shirt?" Janelle asked, pointing at the pearl buttons. "I'm she too." She looked up at the buzzcam, touched her cross pendant, and sent off a prayer for it to keep going. "Okay, everything's up. Let's start with just hanging out a bit, getting loose. Think you can do that?"

It was always better if she had a buffer of material showing the kids looking happy—it was good for splicing in when one of them had a snot bubble during the interview or something—but the kids were doing the kids thing, shuffling around, looking nervous. Nevaeh jumped up behind Janelle and started doing silly dances in the background to make them laugh.

"Thanks, Nevaeh. I'm duly impressed," Janelle said after she had enough recorded giggling. "Now, the interview part. Let's start with . . . you?"

She pointed randomly.

The girl in the formal white dress—Twyla? Tyler?—had apparently prepared her comments in advance, but was struggling to remember them. "To me, UBI is the day when my parents, uh . . . help me figure out how to put the money in, uh . . . places. We save some for college, then, uh . . . look at charities so I can pick one."

Janelle asked, "What charities have you picked?"

Done with her prepared speech, Tori (or whatever) started speaking off the cuff, becoming suddenly charismatic. "Last year I did money for the dolphins. They moved north from the Indian Ocean after it got too hot. This year I want to help all those pets who got lost after, uh, Hurricane Epsilon. Pets should have a home."

"So, first you save some money, and then you give the rest to charity?" Janelle asked.

T-something shook her head. "When I'm done, my parents give me a little to keep because life's not just responsibility, it's also for living."

"Their words?"

T nodded. She added primly, "But I think so, too."

Janelle was impressed. Despite T's difficulty reciting from memory, the girl was surprisingly poised for her age.

"Thanks, T—" Janelle caught herself. "Thank you. That was great."

The girl went back to stand with the other two.

Janelle noticed Nevaeh had gone off somewhere. She frowned. The teacher was still there, so she asked, "Hey, what happened to my sister?"

"She's talking to the older kids," said the teacher. They muttered, "Bless everything that's good. Those kids get so bored. . . ."

"Okay . . ." Janelle said, frowning more. If the teacher wasn't upset, she should probably let it go and get back to work. Right? She didn't like it.

Next came F-something.

"We go to dinner every year," F said. She had a beautiful voice, sweet and unusually mellow. "Everyone goes. Lots of food, everyone shares. I like Chinese. Sometimes my aunt and uncle rent a hotel, but if they don't do it a long time before, everything gets full."

Janelle's attention drifted—not the girl's fault she was boring, she'd probably grow out of it—and she tried to surreptitiously look over the shoulder-height bookcases that marked off the nook. Her peripheral vision caught a bundle of blurs that seemed to be her sister and the older kids, but she couldn't tell what they were doing.

She heard F cough, so she looked back. The girl asked, "Um, was that okay?"

"Yes, fine, wonderful, great," said Janelle. "What's your favorite Chinese dish?"

F said, "Mu shu pancakes with plum sauce."

"Just the pancakes?"

"Yeah!"

"Great, great." Janelle looked to the last girl. Honestly, she couldn't even remember an initial this time. Maybe M. "Hey there . . . you. What's your Windfall Day like?"

M edged forward, eyed the buzzcam warily, and then stood straight to attention as if she were headed to a military parade.

"Mom and Dad go out, so I stay with Shana and Babs."

"Who are they?"

"My sibs."

"Your siblings," Janelle repeated. "Younger or older?"

"Younger." M hushed her voice as if telling a secret. "Mom and Dad leave us money to buy candy at the corner."

"Your parents go out and leave you with your siblings, and then you go to the candy store. And both your siblings are younger than you?" Janelle asked, frowning.

"Yeah," M said happily.

"No one else comes to help?"

"Uh-uh."

Janelle glanced back at the teacher, who looked mortified.

The teacher said, "Mattie, you're making it sound like you're a ragamuffin they leave on the street." They looked to Janelle. "Her mom and dad volunteer to help people get their basic income. They work with a charity that helps indigenous people navigate the system. Right, Mattie?"

Mattie nodded. "Yeah."

"And didn't you tell me your upstairs neighbor comes down to have dinner and watch TV with you?" asked the teacher.

"Yeah," said Mattie, "but I like it when we go get candy."

"Which you do when?" asked the teacher.

"After school."

"In broad daylight? Half a block from home?"

Excitedly, Mattie said, "Yeah!"

The teacher sighed. "Her grandmother was a tribal lawyer. Mattie's parents picked up some of her charity work. They came into class to talk about it."

"What did they talk about?" Janelle asked, feeling a hint of excitement.

The teacher looked hesitant. "Well, there was a thing

about illegally withholding basic income from native women unless they agreed to be sterilized. . . ."

"Yes, I know about that," Janelle said. "Have they found anything else? Rumors keep coming up about forcing people to sign a loyalty oath, but no one's gotten their hands on a copy. Did they say anything about that?"

The teacher looked trapped. "I'm really not an expert. I wouldn't want to say the wrong thing. I can wavve you the name of their org."

Right. It was definitely not That Kind of interview, and she was making everyone uncomfortable. Even if it *were* That Kind of interview, where the heck would she send it? On the international scene, hostility toward indigenous populations was something everyone could agree on. With global warming drowning more and more territory, countries like the US wanted back all the land they'd "given away," no matter how crappy. And anyway, she'd spent half the morning yelling at Nevaeh for this kind of thing.

"That would be great, thanks." Janelle plucked the buzzcam out of the air. "Well, thanks, that's all I need." She put on a huge grin for the kids, and said too cheerfully, "Thanks, you guys! You were swell!" *Swell*? Damn it, kids could smell you trying too hard. Oh well.

The teacher escorted Janelle back into the main classroom, where Nevaeh was gathered by the wall with the cluster of older students, all conferring intensely.

"Hey! Nevaeh!" Janelle called.

Her sister looked up, startled.

Janelle waved her over. As Nevaeh jumped to her feet, Janelle caught a glimpse of her trying to covertly pass something made of black cloth to one of the other kids. Christ on peanut butter toast.

Nevaeh jogged over. Janelle pretended she hadn't seen anything so they could just get out of there.

Olivia

The perfect weather and perfect snow drew crowds of day trippers to Aspen. They whooshed down the slopes with glee, flush with windfalls, ready to zing.

It was a disappointingly beautiful day to miss skiing, but after all, Olivia and her friends had just gotten there. They had plenty of time left to ski. Besides, William had been insisting he had something special planned for weeks. No one was going to argue with William.

Various discussions of contest rules broke out. People who were obsessed with C&C explained things to people who weren't. For instance, since executing a prank could take time, people only had to prove they'd committed their money. Anyone who failed to pull off their scheme would have to surrender their bragging rights and get mocked by C&C's entire audience.

Olivia stopped paying attention so she could watch the distant blots sailing the slopes. She didn't participate in these kinds of events. The person who won was always clever. She wouldn't know what to do.

While people bunched up to discuss their plans, Katie

turned red, snapped at everyone who tried to ask if she was okay, and went into one of the bedrooms with a headache.

Pauline rushed up to Olivia, and pointed to the corner. "Over there, over there, over there! Look! On the ottoman in front of the fireplace!"

Olivia looked. There was a guy with dirty blond hair and a gray headband, watching something on his wrister. Olivia didn't recognize him. She shrugged and shook her head.

Pauline flailed with frustration. Her blonde ponytail bounced around. "That's *the* guy! The one Elsa fucked all over Rome last summer! Remember the story about Trevi? I died!"

"I don't think I heard about it," Olivia said uncomfortably. It wasn't unusual for people to forget to invite her along, which was okay, but it was kind of embarrassing when they forgot that they'd forgotten.

"The guy from Rome! Just don't mention Pop Rocks, right? That's what I keep telling myself. Just don't let it *pop* out! But when I meet him, I know all I'll be thinking is 'Pop Rocks, Pop Rocks, Pop Rocks.' Man, this party is hilarious."

Pauline fumbled in her pockets. She wore the kind of athletic stuff that didn't look expensive unless you knew it was expensive. Her sports wrister had a band made of rubber.

She found what she wanted and offered it to Olivia. "Angie's bones?"

It took Olivia a moment to realize Pauline was asking about the drug, not about real bones. "Oh. I haven't tried it before."

"So do you want it?"

"Yeah, okay."

Olivia took the little white stick that looked like a toothpick and stuck it in her mouth.

"Oh my God! That's a fatal dose!" exclaimed Pauline.

Olivia grabbed at her mouth.

"Kidding," Pauline said. "You're fine. One bone won't hurt you. Unless you've been drinking anything orange! Kidding. You're fine."

Pauline breezed off, whooping to herself. As Olivia watched her go, the world stuttered. An unknown length of time passed, which felt like minutes but also sort of like hours, and then she was back in her body with everything shining. Pauline was across the room.

Through the windows, the mountain slopes grinned at her. The sky giggled, tickled by the feathers of the trees.

Olivia stumbled through the suite, looking for someone familiar. She found Leroy and Freddie with a cute guy in a sweatshirt with long sleeves that covered his wrister. His sweatshirt said Palo Alto. So, Stanford.

"We already talked about this," Freddie said. "Just buying and breaking something doesn't count. You have to be creative."

Leroy said, "Say I commission a giant ice sculpture. Something classy like a woman with huge tits."

Freddie said, "Subtle."

Leroy said, "What the fuck does subtle have to do with it? Pissing is subtle?"

"There's nothing unique about the fact ice melts," said Freddie.

"Pissing is unique?"

Freddie said, "Here's a tip: Don't use ideas that sound like they were made up by a twelve-year-old with a hard-on."

Olivia laughed. Leroy and Freddie looked funny. Leroy was so big. Freddie was so small. There were little white and pink flowers on Freddie's navy button-down, and she was pretty sure the pattern was really there, but the flowers probably weren't jumping.

The boys kept bobbing up and down. Actually, that was the whole world bobbing. Wait, how was she supposed to balance?

Olivia staggered into the Stanford guy, who looked mildly alarmed and helped her back up.

"You can just let her fall on you. She doesn't care," Freddie said. "She just likes attention."

"If you put her hand on your dick, she'll probably go automatically," said Leroy.

The word *automatically* was funny, so she laughed. The Stanford guy gave her a concerned look from the corner of his eye. Oh. Wasn't he sweet.

The Stanford guy cleared his throat. "Uh. What it makes me think of is Ai Wei Wei. He's a Chinese artist from last century who was protesting in the . . . nineties, I think? He took three photographs of himself smashing a Han dynasty urn. I won't get into specifics, because you can't really get it unless you know how things work in China, but it was a *huge* deal in art *and* politics. The photographs are in the Guggenheim."

"Artists are assholes," Leroy said.

Freddie smiled at the Stanford guy, flirting. Idly, he toyed with the charms hanging from his wrister. "So you're saying that shouldn't count as waste?"

The Stanford guy agreed. "By destroying the urn, he created something else that was possibly even *more* important." He paused. "But *afterward,* a lot of new artists did the same thing, for no reason except it made this other guy famous."

"Yeah," said Leroy. "Because artists are assholes."

"And then all you've got is a shit-ton of broken urns." Freddie's charms jangled.

"Exactly," said the Stanford guy.

Olivia wobbled. The Stanford guy caught her again, and kept his hand on her shoulder this time to help her stay up. Freddie rolled his eyes.

"Uh," the Stanford guy continued. "There's also the old story about Cleopatra. She makes a bet with Marc Anthony about who can spend the most on a meal. She serves him a pot of vinegar, takes the world's most expensive pearl, and"—he made a fist with his free hand—"crushes it into the vinegar."

"That's apocryphal," said Freddie dismissively. His flirty smile disappeared; he stopped playing with the charms on his wrister, and stuck his hand in his pocket.

"What do you always do that for?" Leroy asked. "He's just telling a fucking story. It's an idea. We're talking. It's not a goddamn history lesson."

Freddie shrugged. "I believe we should strive for accuracy."

The Stanford guy tried again. "My problem is: How are we defining waste? Literally—as in junkyards? Or are we trying to screw people over? Does the whole thing become performance art—"

Leroy interrupted, "No, I know what you do. You get the money in cash, then pay some guy minimum wage to dig a bunch of holes and bury it a hundred dollars at a time."

"You'd have to pay by the hole, not the hour," said Freddie.

"Why?"

"Because otherwise he'd just work slowly." Freddie went on tiptoe to smack Leroy's forehead. "Come on, Lee. Think."

Leroy turned red. "Shut up."

The Stanford guy looked at Olivia with his eyes wide. "Are you okay—?"

Then Don said, "Hey, Livvy Liv."

Olivia blinked at Don.

Oh, she wasn't with the other guys anymore. No Freddie, no Leroy. No Stanford guy, which was kind of too bad because he seemed nice.

She was in the kitchen with Don now. Okay.

Don was doing his usual charisma thing: winking, joking, flirting, making fancy bows as he handed out drinks. His clothes were perfectly tailored and perfectly ironed. That was Don for you. Freddie said Don dressed up because he was trying to compensate for having less money than the rest of them, but he didn't say it around Don. Olivia didn't recognize the brand of Don's wrister, but it looked nice.

He finished handing out drinks to the people waiting, and turned to Olivia. "Want a drink, Livvy Liv? How about a Paloma?"

"Yeah, okay." A bright light flashed in her eye. "Oh!"

Don frowned in concern. "Everything okay?"

"Just a message," Olivia said, blinking it away.

Don ran one finger along the band of her wrister. His other hand cupped the side of her face. "The flash shouldn't be bright enough to hurt you. Need me to help fix it, Liv?" When she didn't answer, he asked, "What'd the message say?"

"Oh, I don't know. . . . I didn't really read it. . . ." Olivia mumbled. "It was the . . . money person. The deposit got stuck, so it's going to be late."

"Stuck?"

"In the maze. On the way to my vault."

Don tried to keep his face neutral, but a flash of resentment passed through his eyes. "Ah, your vault account. Personal? Just curious."

"Yeah, it's my vault," Olivia said. She wasn't sure what he wanted.

"Ah," Don said. "We closed the family vault. Insurance fees snowball every time some Indian hacker snatches a penny. . . ." He trailed off. Smiling, he said fondly, "I'm being silly. You don't need to worry about knowing this stuff, do you, Liv?"

He bopped her on the nose.

"Poor Liv," he said. "We'll always find someone to take care of you."

He moved his lips toward her face. She felt the heat of his breath. His gaze was pointed straight down her dress. He slid one hand down her hip.

"Settle a bet, Lovely Liv?"

Olivia said, "I guess?"

She felt unsteady. She tried to move, but her legs were everywhere, and they forgot how to stand.

Don caught her. His hand slipped under her dress.

"See, I think Don Julio Real is the best tequila, but Elsa's been telling everyone to drink Tres Cuatro Cinco. I'm right, though, aren't I, Little Liv?"

His hand moved up her thigh.

"You're right," Olivia said, although she didn't really remember the question. She forced a thought through her shining brain. She realized she had a way to get him to stop. "Can I have that Paloma?"

He looked sad, and waited for a second, as if hoping she'd suddenly change her mind. He pulled his hand back. She heard the flick of elastic snapping back into place.

"You bet, Lively Livvy."

Don grabbed a bottle. He wagged his eyebrows at her as he tossed it hand to hand. Olivia giggled uncomfortably whenever he caught her eye, but that was okay because he probably just thought she was flirting.

She wanted to go sit down again so she could stare at the grinning mountains and the tickling trees.

Someone shouted, "—all enormous assholes!"

The room fell quiet. Everyone turned to the door. Standing by the piano, there was a plumpish neut with light stubble and who was wearing a well-fitted high school letterman jacket.

"This is unreal," said the neut in the jacket. "Un-fucking-real. I can't—I can't believe I came here."

"Mo!" shouted a pretty girl in a long-sleeved jumpsuit, pushing through the crowd. "No one's judging you! It's just a game."

"Like hell it is," said Mo. "You think anyone who *uses* their UBI doesn't know exactly what this is? You think we don't know exactly what—who!—you're talking about? I'm not a waste! No one's a waste! You actually *call* it bread and circuses. You *admit* you're the ones who run the Colosseum!"

Someone muttered something about class warfare.

Mo glared them down. "You know, *most* rich people aren't like this. *Most* rich people think this kind of thing is disgusting. This isn't just about being rich. It's about being rich and *cruel*." They turned back to their friend. "Carrie, I *know* you're a good person. I don't know how you can be here and be a good person—but that's for you to figure out."

"Mo—"

"The rest of you," they said, surveying the stunned room, "if you believe you're a good person, think long and hard about getting out of here. And if you don't, then *maybe* you're *wrong*."

Someone shouted, "Shut up, asshole!"

"Attention whore," said someone else.

Mo shrugged and went for the door.

"Mo!" Carrie shouted, running after them.

The door shut behind them.

There were long seconds of quiet.

Leroy exclaimed, "I volunteer to waste my oobi trying to get the stick out of that ass!"

The quiet broke into sound like a clap, and everyone went back to talking.

Sarah

The Utah rain settled into a very light but cold drizzle, the kind people complained about but still ventured out in without umbrellas. They drove to lunch, took their kids to dentist appointments, and stood in line to buy groceries. For most people, it wasn't much but small talk.

Sarah and Agnes walked quietly for a while. Agnes could only go so fast on little legs, and Sarah had to pause now and then to let her stomach settle. A few more groups passed until finally they were all the way in back with Molly and her kids, who always brought up the rear.

When the rain paused for a bit, Molly stopped them to make sure they were drinking plenty of water. She gave out snacks—homemade granola bars in a wet plastic bag. The bars were dry, but Sarah's sense of smell was so overwhelming that the bars still tasted metallic like the fallen rain.

Molly set a hand on Sarah's shoulder before going on. "You should know, honey, we all see how hard things have been for you. Some women talk a lot"—she glanced down the road, implying Sarah's sister-wives—"but most people know to trust what they see. They know not to give credence to the kind of person who'll tell you the sky is yellow while you're looking up at blue."

Sarah couldn't make a smile reach her eyes, but she tried.

Molly asked if they wanted to walk with her and her kids, but neither Agnes nor Sarah wanted to be with anyone else right then. When the group moved on, the two of them lingered where they were, giving Molly a little time to get ahead.

Agnes looked up at Sarah cautiously like a deer eyeing a hunter. "I'm sorry, Sarah."

Sarah shrugged, embarrassed. "You don't need to be sorry. I didn't mean to yell at you."

Immediately, Agnes lit up, happy again. "It's okay! You just got going. I know I can be annoying."

Sarah hesitated, uncomfortable with how quick Agnes was to bury her hurt.

"Agnes . . ." Sarah said. "You're a lot better at being nice than a lot of people. You're definitely better at being nice than me. A lot of people are good at *acting* nice, but it's better to *be* nice. You have a good heart. The world would be a lot better if people had hearts like yours whether or not they keep sweet."

Agnes ducked her head, looking flushed. "Mom says desserts are better if you mix in at least one thing that isn't sweet."

Sarah smiled. "Once when I was, I'm not sure, maybe five years old, when I was learning to cook from Gran, I put sugar instead of salt into the tomato sauce."

"Tomato sauce is good with sugar," Agnes said.

"Not this much. It was a *lot* of sugar. I started crying because I thought she'd be mad. Gran just looked at it and said, 'We can fix this, easy.' She got flour and eggs and so on and she made"—Sarah paused for effect—"tomato cupcakes."

Agnes giggled. "Were they any good?"

"Yeah, we made them on purpose sometimes before Gran died. I should make them again." Sarah frowned, thinking, and then slowly shook her head as if the air were thick with worries. "I just wonder how you know when things are too spoiled to fix."

"I bet Mom would say nothing's too spoiled to use for something."

"Yeah," Sarah agreed, "but I bet she throws away bad chicken."

Agnes snorted. She waved a hand in front of her nose at an imaginary spoiled chicken smell. Her expression turned suddenly thoughtful, and she gave Sarah an assessing sideways glance.

"Do you hate Faith and Dorcas and Mary?"

"No. Maybe. I don't know." Sarah crossed her arms protectively over her chest. "I don't think it matters."

"Do you think they won't help with the baby?"

"I don't know. I'm not planning on it."

Agnes looked at her the way someone looks at a puppy with a broken leg. "I think that's sad."

Sarah said, "It happens."

Agnes's look didn't change. "It can still be sad."

There wasn't much else to say about that. They started walking again.

The last part of the trip seemed to stretch forever. They walked around glass remnants and a spray of dried red on the side of the road where there had been a car accident. Someone spat at them from a car window, but it blew back into his face. Agnes giggled about that for a long time, and then started guessing how the wind would blow spit from the other cars that passed them. Fortunately, they never found out whether any of her guesses were right.

When the Service Liaison Office finally came into sight, Sarah sighed with relief. As always, the large square building was surrounded by heretical "mainstream" Mormons. It was late in the day now and many of the protestors had gone home. Those remaining seemed tired. A few women sat in camping chairs. A line of empty Diet Pepsi cans and water bottles stood in front of a drinks cooler near their feet.

Earlier today, it would have been fiery, the heretics waving banners and shouting for the women to: *Liberate yourselves from abuse! Your children deserve better! God wants better for you! Break free!*

Most of the prophet's women would have recoiled, giving the protestors a wide berth as they clutched their infants and hid their children behind their skirts. Some would have shouted back: *I'm a wife, not a victim! Child stealers! We won't let you steal our children again!*

While the shouting volleyed back and forth, the quiet women would pass swiftly behind the ones fighting back. Some whispered rebukes: *Keep sweet!* Others thanked them: *For speaking up, for keeping the protestors busy, for defending the truth.*

As Sarah and Agnes neared the entrance, the protestors perked up, picking up their signs. Two of the women in camping chairs stood up. A boy around Agnes's age shouted before they were quite in range. "Kids should be kids! Don't go back!"

The adult protestors pitched in with various chants. Agnes pulled Sarah's sleeve with alarm. "I don't want to go past."

"It'll be fine."

"He looked at me. He was talking to me."

"He just saw you're both kids. It's okay, Agnes, you've done this before."

Agnes whimpered. "They've never been looking at *me* before!"

"Just pass on the outside of me," Sarah said.

A "mainstream" Mormon woman called to Sarah, "It's not right what they did to you. Get your baby somewhere safe!"

"Oh, *stop it*," snarled Sarah. "You're scaring my cousin. If you really want to help, if that's really why you're doing this, then stop yelling at us. Shouting is not help!"

Both Agnes and the woman flinched at the same time, and Sarah realized she'd been screaming without even noticing. The woman she'd been yelling at looked shocked. Sarah felt a flush on her face. Her heart was racing. She clutched Agnes's hand and rushed her inside.

UBI DAY: AFTERNOON

Hannah

The wind and snow screamed at each other, too equally matched for either to win.

All Hannah could think of was how long it would take Abigail to park and get to the house. Luckily, it was harder than it looked to get from the driveway to the front door if you didn't know the shortcut. The ice would help too.

Elizabeth noticed Hannah's face. "What's wrong?"

The question broke Hannah out of stasis. "Sorry. You can't stay. You should go now. Use the back door from the kitchen."

"What? Why?"

"The boys and I have to leave," Hannah said. There wasn't time for more excuses. "We'll go out through the back door too. Don't lock it."

Hannah felt the weight of the checkbook in her hand and remembered it was there. She grabbed her purse from the rack and started stuffing it with the contents of the drawer, all the things she kept close-to-hand in case they needed to bolt.

She zipped the purse, hoping she'd gotten everything as she ran to the stairs. To Elizabeth, she repeated, "We need to leave now. You can play with the boys if you want. After we get out."

"You're panicking," Elizabeth said. "Don't be embarrassed. Most people panic in crisis situations. Tell me what's going on."

Hannah felt her face go red. She had a quick surge of anger, but it splashed away again into the clamor of urgency.

She shoved her emotions away. Her hands kept moving. "My ex-wife is here. She broke Jake's rib last time she found us. I want to get him out of here before she can do something like that again. I'm sorry. We need to leave immediately. I can pull an extra month's rent out of my oobi to compensate for your trouble."

Elizabeth seemed unperturbed; actually, her eyes had brightened. "Have you changed anything in here?"

"What?" Hannah's hands paused for half a second before resuming. "No. You can rent it out again as soon as we go. Try not to let her know you've seen us."

"Stop, listen to me. I handled worse than this in the army. Go upstairs and hide with your boys. They'll feel better if you're there. I'll handle this, I promise."

Hannah protested, "Mrs. Allen—"

Elizabeth pointed up the stairs. "Go."

Hannah looked between Elizabeth and the door. Time was draining away. She almost certainly couldn't get the boys out cleanly at this point. If Elizabeth could earn them a few minutes, she'd take them.

Hannah nodded. "Okay." She ran to the foot of the stairs. "Boys! Do what we practiced. Jake, remember, please. I need you to do this."

Sudden pounding on the door made both women jump. Hannah fled up the stairs, but instead of going into the boys' room, she hid in the shadows behind the balustrade. Hopefully, they'd be starting to barricade their door now. More importantly, if Elizabeth failed, Hannah couldn't let her face Abigail's anger alone. She knew how to take the brunt of it, especially if she didn't have to protect Jake from trying to help at the same time.

Elizabeth took a minute to collect herself, seemingly unhurried by Abigail's frantic banging and shouting. The racket was loud enough to cover the sound of the kids moving their furniture. Thank God. Hannah's heart was a rabbit, thrashing in her chest.

Calmly, Elizabeth opened the door. Abigail was caught mid-motion, stumbling to catch herself.

Abigail looked messy even from far away. Her hair was uneven, longer on one side than the other. Her old T-shirt didn't fit. Just seeing her spiked Hannah's anxiety so much that for a moment her vision was pulsing and dim;

she clutched the rail to keep from falling.

Abigail bellowed, "My wife is in here!"

"Yes, I heard you shouting," said Elizabeth. "I don't know who told you that your wife was living here, and I don't know why they said it, but this is my property."

"She's not here?" Abigail asked, seeming confused. Her eyes were too bright. She was on something. "You live here?"

"It's my property," Elizabeth repeated. "Look around this place. Anything here look like your wife's? No? That's because it's mine. And now you need to go."

"Then let me see for myself," Abigail said. "Let me in."

Abigail wasn't a large woman, but she moved with a weighty swagger that cowed almost everyone. She claimed she'd learned it during the year she worked at the deli that turned out to be a mob front. Abigail swung her shoulder toward Elizabeth as if she were going to bash into her. Abigail had seen large men flinch when she did that. Elizabeth didn't.

Abigail stopped before actually shoving into Elizabeth, seeming confused again. "My wife's in there," she repeated.

"This is my house. You need to go."

"But my wife's in there."

"No, she's not. This is *my* house. I don't know what about this is so hard for you to understand. Now, are you going to get out, or does this need to get serious?"

Abigail blinked a few times, but didn't move.

Elizabeth reached casually underneath her bulky sweater and pulled out a gun.

Hannah nearly gave herself away with a yelp. Elizabeth trained the thing on the ground, but her demeanor made it clear that she could aim perfectly well if she needed to.

"I'm Elizabeth Allen. This house is mine. I am not your wife. Do you understand?"

Abigail stared fixedly at the gun, eyes bulging. Hannah felt torn between taking a mean satisfaction in that and worrying that humiliation would goad Abigail even further and get them all killed.

"Say it back to me," Elizabeth said.

"You're not Hannah."

"And this is my house."

"It's your house." Abigail frowned again. She shook her head as if she were trying to clear it. "Have you seen her?"

"Who?"

"My wife."

"I have never seen your wife," Elizabeth said. "Get out of here, and don't come back."

Abigail's frown deepened. She looked between the gun and Elizabeth as if they were a mystery she couldn't solve. Suddenly, she blinked, and it was as if she were seeing the gun for the first time.

Her cartoonishly frightened expression returned. She held up her hands. "Should I repeat . . . ?"

Elizabeth made a little shrug. "Sure."

"I won't come back." Abigail backed up a step, then paused, trembling. Her expression changed to heartbreaking sincerity. "If you see my wife, tell her I miss her. We have two sons, her and me. Tell her I miss our sons."

Looking at that miserable face, all Hannah could think of was the obstetrics ward where she'd sat with Abigail both times, watching her pant and sweat, worrying for the babies and wishing there was something she could do to stop her wife's pain. It hadn't been so bad the second time, with Isaiah, but laboring the first time with Jake had broken Abigail's tailbone and there had been nothing Hannah could do to make it better. She remembered how Abigail's sweaty grimace had become a glossy flush once she was holding the baby, even through her pain and exhaustion. Hannah remembered having thought she was seeing what absolute love looked like. She hated herself for breaking Abigail and the children apart, and she hated herself for not getting out somehow as soon as Isaiah was born (because how could she wish she'd left earlier if it meant she had no Isaiah?)—and there was still a shard of love for Abigail lodged in her heart because how could she ever completely stop loving someone who had come together with her to make new life?

Elizabeth said nothing.

Abigail blinked a few more times, eyes clearly wet, and then backed away.

Janelle

The Chicago air was dry but tense, waiting for something to shift. Storm clouds thickened, threatening to tantrum. The afternoon was dimming early. It wasn't the weather for thunderstorms, but the crackling anticipation felt the same.

When Janelle and Nevaeh were on the train again, Janelle asked, "Did you give one of your shirts to those middle-school students?"

"They asked."

"Oh, *did* they? With what prompting? Out of nowhere? Gosh, *do you have a vulgar T-shirt promoting a political viewpoint I've never even heard of?*"

"They knew about reparations," Nevaeh said. "Well, one of them did."

"The one you gave the shirt?"

"Uh, he said his mom would hit the roof if she saw he had a T-shirt with the f-word on it."

Janelle snorted.

"Kids *die* in the US *every day,*" Nevaeh said. "Tropical fevers and storms and abuse and hunger and neglect. It's stupid to worry about whether they know the word *fuck*."

Passing on the bait, Janelle said, "You should have let me handle the kids. Some parents get mad when you ask kids their pronouns these days, especially little ones."

"The 'no asking pronouns' thing is stupid," Nevaeh said. "I *am* a kid, and I love every damn time I get to say I'm a girl."

Janelle felt a twitch of concern. "Are you getting shit from other kids?"

"Nah. No one cares if I'm a swap sister."

"Don't use that slang, please. It's trans, cis, and nonbinary."

"Whatever. There's nothing wrong with swap, stat, and squiggle."

"Can't you at least use neut?"

"Sure, then I'll meet up with the flappers at the drive-in for a tubular rave, qween," said Nevaeh. "I *like* swap, stat, and squiggle."

"They're very . . . teenager," said Janelle, meaning juvenile, obnoxious and mildly clever.

"Plus we also have squib, squee, and squonk."

"You're giving me a headache. Okay, tell me."

"Squib is no gender, like agender. Squee is extreme gender, way too gonzo for a squiggle. A squonk is sick of it, like *I don't even want to talk about this, go squonk yourself*."

"Can you be squonk about your whole life?" Janelle grumbled.

Nevaeh shrugged and looked away.

Janelle wasn't sure what was wrong, so she hopped to another joke. "How about *square* for people who just want to use trans, cis, and nonbinary?"

"Huh," said Nevaeh, warming a little. "So last century. I like it. I'll contact the teen slang board."

"Please do." Switching to a serious tone, Janelle said, "While you're with me at work, please let me take the lead, okay?"

Nevaeh stuck out her tongue. "I should make you trade shirts with me in exchange."

Janelle stuck hers out in return. "Only if you don't want to go over to Deja's until the snow's all melted."

Nevaeh leaned over Janelle's shoulder to look at the map she had open on her phone. "How many interviews left to go?"

"Oh, dear child," Janelle said. "So, so many."

Interior, the bank.

Person wearing horrible yellow heels: At least you get back a little of what the IRS steals.

Person with sweaty face: It all goes in savings. It makes me feel more secure.

Person using service dog: My great-grandmother would have slapped me. She *hated* banks. She never set foot in one after they lost all her money.

Teller with shiny hair: January fifteenth is our busiest day all year. People come in who've never had anything but a postal account.

Janelle: What do you think is bringing customers back to private banking?

Teller: We've worked hard over the past decade to restore consumer confidence in the banking industry. People have come to realize they can trust our security and anti-fraud protocols. Postal accounts can cover some basics, but customers want the advantages a real bank can provide—

Nevaeh: Well, they shouldn't. For-profit banking is always worse for the poor.

Janelle: Oh my God.

Teller: I don't know where you're getting your information, young person, but we pride ourselves on our mobile-class programs.

Janelle: Nevaeh, go wait by the potted plants, and don't bother people. Sorry. She's my sister. You know teens.

As soon as they were on the sidewalk, Nevaeh said, "You know mobile class is a euphemism for *poor*."

"Yeah, but I don't see why that needed to be pointed out just then," said Janelle. "Don't do that again, Nevaeh. This shirt thing is lighthearted. Don't make me get all serious."

Nevaeh kept pestering. "Don't you *miss* fighting for justice?"

"Ha!" Janelle said, then explained, "Sorry, that phrasing is just a little retired superhero."

"I remember from when I was little—you were *on fire*. You *never* thought things were done."

"Is that a Thanksgiving joke?" Janelle asked, thinking of burned turkey.

"I didn't see you much growing up—"

"Because I never claimed I was a good cook," Janelle went on.

Neveah made a frustrated noise. "Listen."

"All right, all right."

Neveah continued, "I didn't see you much growing up."

"Sorry. I was always running around those days."

"*No,* I mean, I didn't see you much, but when I *did,* you were fiery! You were always *chasing* something."

"My own tail," Janelle grumbled.

"Come *on.* Be *serious.*"

Interior, the drugstore.

Nevaeh: We're stopping here?

Janelle: I need tampons.

Nevaeh: The buzzcam's on.

Janelle: No reason not to grab some filler interviews. For instance—

Surprised employee who'd been mopping the hair-care aisle: Yeah, I get double time for the holiday, but I'd rather be sleeping. You can make them give you time off if you pick up your check in person, but I've had mine by mail since before graduating high school.

Janelle: Great! Thanks! And where are the feminine products?

Surprised employee: Over there, ma'am, near the tanning lotions.

The wind had gotten louder again, so Nevaeh waited to start grilling Janelle until they were on the train. She asked, "Is UBI why you stopped talking to Dad?"

"Huh? Oh," Janelle said. "Not really. It would have happened anyway."

"I remember you arguing the last night you were home."

"Dad was . . . A lot of doctors in specialty medicine didn't like UBI. They were never going to stop earning mountains of money, but no one thinks enough is enough. If I've learned anything from interviews, it's that. Dad in particular—he could *not* handle risks to his income, big *or* small. I mean, I get it. When I was a kid, he'd wake up from nightmares about us losing our house the way his parents lost theirs. One of Dad's friends from medical school lost a lot of money in a breach during the quantum transition . . . then after the blockchain crash, Dad started getting *really* paranoid. . . ."

Janelle trailed off.

"Yeah?" prompted Nevaeh.

Janelle shrugged. "We still talked. I just stopped visiting. I lived across the country anyway. I wavved every couple weeks, remember? It hasn't been *that* long."

"I remember," Nevaeh said. "I never had anything to say."

"You could have told me about school."

"No way. My *activist big sister* didn't want to hear about *schoolwork*."

Janelle hesitated. "I hate to say it, but you're probably right. Slowing down was really hard for me back then."

Interior, the extremely fancy toy store.

Janelle: Hello, youngster. Did your parents get you a toy today?

Sandy-haired child who keeps squealing: I got this sword! See? This sword! My parents got it for me. Look, it goes swoosh! Swish! Yeah! Whoosh, whoosh!

Nevaeh: Oh no! I am stabbed! Soon, I shall die!

Squealing kid: [so much more squealing]

Janelle and Nevaeh left the toy store through the back entrance so they could walk through the indoor mall—and of course, they were immediately drenched in sweat. During winter, half the businesses in Chicago were heated to blasting, because heaven forbid anywhere should ever be a reasonable temperature.

Through crowds of UBI Day shoppers, Janelle and Nevaeh glimpsed store windows filled with goods competing to win just a little of all that shiny new UBI money. Smooth-faced mannequin heads wore state-of-the-art masks with sweat-absorbing fabric and high-quality voice filters. Full-body mannequins wore flowery wardrobes from upcoming spring lines, which were released earlier and earlier every year for anyone impractical or impatient enough to sacrifice closet space for fantasies of warmer weather. Some windows looked in on jumbled racks of sequin-banded wristers for adolescent girls that broke in a week; others displayed a single elegant bauble on white velvet, gilded by spotlights. And, splashed across everything, blaring like a headache, was that ridiculous bright yellow with which today's fad-shionistas were assaulting the eyes of the innocent.

"Okay, so," Nevaeh said. "Go over it with me again. UBI got started because everyone was scared after Winter Night."

"Right," said Janelle.

"Because they were afraid of nuclear winter."

"Right."

"Even though it was summer."

"One of life's great ironies."

"And you were living in D.C."

"Technically commuting from Virginia."

"And everyone was so glad 'to be alive when dawn impearled, they gathered up to save the world'? Like the poem?"

"Sure," said Janelle. Pursing her lips, she added, "You *were* around for this. What's going on with you?"

"I didn't used to care about the news."

"Yeah, you were little."

"*You* started watching the news when you were three."

"Mom used to say that, but I think I just wanted to stay up late."

"I just want to understand what's going on! I just want to make things better."

"So say we all!" chanted Janelle.

Nevaeh looked hurt.

Janelle said, "Sorry, sweetie. That's just . . . one of those hard things about the world. Making things better doesn't always work. I'm glad you care. It's good to care."

Near mall entrance, interior, because "person on the actual street" would be ridiculous in this weather.

Janelle: Oh my God. *Why are they playing that fucking C&C show on the intercom!!!*

Nevaeh (egregiously overacting): *Janni!* Such language!

Janelle (to person with knobbly wool sweater who stopped to look at the camera): Hey there. Any thoughts about UBI today?

Person with knobbly wool sweater: UBI? It's the worst thing that ever happened to this country. My sister had a little bakery, mostly breakfast sweets. She made it all herself. It took just *eighteen months* for it to collapse. *Eighteen months.* Ten years of her life gone so some asshole can avoid getting a job.

Shouty person with dramatic diphthongs: *That's* my brother-in-law! He's the *asshole* who *won't* get a job. At least he *used* to *work* at a drive-through. Now he uses *air freshener* instead of doing laundry. He gets *furious* if you ask him to do *anything,* even *clean* his own *bathroom.* I think it's *some* kind of *hoarding* thing. I don't even *try* to get him to *leave the house* any—

Very small and sticky child (reaching for Nevaeh's shirt, unfortunately at breast height): Pretty!

Embarrassed parent (pulling child a few steps back): Sorry, he thinks your shirt is pretty. He likes the buttons.

Janelle (to embarrassed parent): Any thoughts on UBI for the camera?

Embarrassed parent: Not really . . . I don't really pay attention to politics.

Once the person in the knobbly wool sweater, the shouty person, and the embarrassed parent wandered off (toddler appropriately in tow), Janelle plucked the buzzcam out of the air and put it in her purse.

Nevaeh watched with her arms folded. "So, it took there almost being a war for things to really change last time."

"More or less," Janelle agreed.

"So then what do we do now? *Wait* for another *disaster*?" Nevaeh asked plaintively. "Because there's so much still wrong."

Janelle sighed. "I know."

Someone cleared their throat. Janelle startled, and then noticed there was someone waiting. Janelle realized she'd seen them earlier, reading a battered paper book while sitting across the hall in their wheelchair. They still held the book in their lap, a finger pressed between pages to mark their place.

On a hunch, Janelle retrieved the buzzcam from her purse. "Hello. How are you?"

"Fine." They pointed to the buzzcam. "I'd like to say something."

Interior, mall. Again.

Wheelchair user with old paper book (in a steady voice as if they'd been rehearsing): I had friends who died. When their services were cut for oobi. Everyone lost their in-home care. Izzy had a seizure, and Jodi stopped breathing one night. It hurt old people, too—Kids—We got lumped together and dumped. Like all our problems are the same and we all need cash. But cash doesn't solve everything. No one's supposed to need free school lunch anymore, but some kids, their parents blow all their money. What about them? People like to say—I bet you've heard it today—people say disabled people, poor people "love oobi." I get angry. It hurts. Just—remember that when you decide what people ought to hear.

The person left quickly afterward. Janelle and Nevaeh stayed quiet for a few minutes, watching after them.

"We should get going again," Janelle said. "I can still get in more interviews before I need to get back to call my friend."

"Who *is* your friend?" Nevaeh asked. "Are you dating someone?"

Janelle laughed. "No, no, it's my friend Dynasty—I met her doing an interview the first year of UBI. She owns a trailer on a tiny little piece of land in Missouri. She makes pots. I call her every year, but you're usually in your room."

"Oh. You don't talk to your friends very often."

Janelle paused, surprised at the conversational turn. "No. Well, people get busy."

Once they were sitting on the train again, Nevaeh gave Janelle a plaintive look. "Things are going to get worse than they are now. Climate refugees are going to keep coming."

"Yes."

"And there's the tropical fevers and the acid killing the fish and all those old mine collapses in Appalachia."

Janelle mumbled, "At least they're getting sun in December these days."

Nevaeh waved her hands urgently. "We can't just let all that go!"

"We can't fix it either. Nevaeh, seriously. What's up with you?" Janelle ran through her mental list of "basic kid needs" and realized she was one down. "Are you hungry? When did you last eat?"

Interior, casual dining chain.

Server with headband and retro browline glasses (delivering order of fries): Honestly, I think people like making a big deal out of things. No offense. If people enjoy arguing, that's fine, I guess. For ninety-nine percent of us, life's basically the same as always. [Pausing to adjust glasses] My cousin throws a great windfall party, though. I'm headed over after my shift.

Janelle: Wait, Nevaeh, how are you *already* finished eating?

Server (laughing): I'll take care of your tray. Enjoy the rest of your day.

"UBI *itself* causes so many problems," Nevaeh resumed when they left. "Do you know how many people there are without IDs or addresses?"

"Still quite a few, apparently."

"A lot of them are Black. And felons—some people

are trying to take away their UBI."

"And Americans love throwing Black people in jail."

"Exactly!" said Nevaeh. "And there hasn't been as much capital growth in Black communities as they thought, and no one knows why."

"Racism."

"But they don't know how it works! It's—like—They want to take basic income away from *all immigrants,* even after they get citizenship."

"People really hate immigrants. Sometimes even White ones."

"And right now employers are only automating the bad jobs they can't fill, but what about when they keep going? When no one can get jobs?"

"Soap operas will get a lot more popular."

"But it's like you wrote in your essays! You knew this stuff would happen!"

"My essays." Resentfully, Janelle said, "You know the newsletter where I had that column added exactly zero to my paycheck."

"I *like* your essays. You could go back to a job like that. We don't have to stay in our neighborhood."

"You'd have to move high schools."

"It's so expensive here. If we weren't in a big city, you could quit working for the aggregators."

Nevaeh was too worked up to notice they'd reached

their next stop. Janelle called out while Nevaeh walked blithely ahead. "Hey, hey, stop. We're at the hospital."

They stomped snow off their boots under the overhang and pushed their way into the rotating door.

"All this because of my essays?" Janelle shook her head in confusion as they entered the lobby. "I don't understand why you're digging into this. Last year, you stayed home and ate ramen. What is going on with you?"

Nevaeh burst into tears.

"Nevaeh?"

"I ruined your life!"

"What?"

"I ruined your life and I'm so sorry and I didn't mean to but I did and I'm sorry!"

Janelle was temporarily stunned into silence.

"You didn't ruin my life," Janelle said. "Maybe Sky Sun Air ruined my life—"

The sobs got so much louder.

"Sorry! I didn't mean that. It was just a stupid joke."

Nevaeh put her face in her hands and ran into a corridor.

"Nevaeh! Nevaeh! Damn it."

For a moment, Janelle couldn't move. Here she was, failing Nevaeh again. When she'd first arrived to take care of Nevaeh—this little girl she hadn't seen in person for how many years?—she'd resolved to let their relationship grow into its own thing, not try to replace Mom and Dad. She and Nevaeh were never going to have a "normal" dynamic. Why fake it? Except then she had to figure out how to parent without being *a* parent. Balancing strict and silly and supportive—and most important, *stable,* even though doing one thing in one place was pretty much the number one thing Janelle had always wanted to avoid.

Most of the time, everything seemed to work pretty well. But then sometimes it didn't, and it made Janelle wonder if the good times were an illusion. Maybe she was always screwing up and didn't even know enough to see it.

Janelle touched her cross pendant. "Could you be a little more helpful, God?" Remembering she'd caused enough trouble being flippant, she added, "I mean, please. I could use some help."

Her body remembered to move, and she rushed after her sister.

Olivia

The ski lodges were bursting with money, but more crowds meant more risks. The mood among staff began to dampen. A young man took a bad fall, and died on the way to the hospital. Returning to the resort, the man's wife and his parents fought bitterly in the lobby about some old resentment that was about to become a proxy for who should take the blame for the young man's death.

Olivia found herself in a group with Elsa and some other people. Her Paloma was gone. She had a bottle of something bitter that was full to the neck.

"Why don't people have a sense of humor anymore?" Elsa scoffed. "It's called eye-ron-eeeee. I-R-O-N-Y. Fucking drama queens."

Elsa was pissed. The curled edge of her layered bob swung back and forth as she shook her head. She wore a backless shirt with a Georgetown logo even though she went to Harvard. The diamond bezel on her wrister glittered.

"Apparently, Mo uses their oobi to offset their tuition at Dartmouth," Pauline said.

"Mo," repeated Olivia with a giggle; it made her lips into an interesting shape.

Pauline seemed to think Olivia was asking a question. She answered, "The one in the varsity jacket who shouted at everyone."

"Who cares how Mo uses it? It's irrelevant." Elsa's hand knifed the air. "No one's telling them what to do with *their* money. Why does Mo think they have any right to tell *us*?"

Pauline raised her hands defensively. "Hey, I'm just saying what I heard."

"Poisonous, self-centered entitlement," said Elsa. "It's not enough for liberals to snatch other people's money and give it away. No. They have to control what everyone *does* with it. What jokes they make. What they *think*. It's not about freedom. If it were about freedom, they'd leave us alone. But they *don't*. They *attack*. Mo the 'debate champion' is allowed to tell us we're assholes for entering a contest, but what do you think would happen if someone went and told Mo they shouldn't use their money for Dartmouth? Asked them: Why aren't *you* donating it? Why don't you find some Ecuadorian refugee who's starving and getting raped and watching her kids stroke out in the heat? Liberals would fucking freak out. They'd call you a fascist. You'd be lucky to get out alive. But *Mo* can just come and yell at *us*, no problem."

"Take a breath, Elsa," Freddie said. He angled his face away from Elsa so she couldn't see him roll his eyes.

Elsa's face was turning red under her foundation. She jabbed a finger, probably at an imaginary Mo. "You know what UBI does? It pays for cults to keep making child brides. It keeps addicts in cocaine when they're living on the streets. But no one wants to talk about *that*. No, ninety percent of your freshman floor wants to talk about *The mega-rich are parasites* and *If I had that much money, I'd donate it all to African rhinos and make a pilgrimage to the drowned city of Basra to self-flagellate in front of the endangered fish*—and really? Would they? Because I don't see *them* giving up everything *they* have. If they want to blame people like me for children getting skin cancer in Indonesia, then they should take a good look back at themselves. They want all the goodies of riding along with our economy? They want to go to school with the big girls in the Ivies? Go for it, but they better remember those tumors are theirs, too. Hypocrites. Self-righteous mosquitos with the moral sophistication of toddlers."

"Been having trouble with your classmates?" asked Freddie with a smirk.

"Not at all. I know how to keep my mouth shut around people I can't trust," Elsa said.

Leroy laughed. He singsonged, "Par-a-noid," which was a thing they'd done to Elsa in high school.

"I don't even *enter* shit like this," Elsa said. "I *donate* my UBI. But they have no fucking right to judge me either way."

"Did your dorm build you a guillotine?" asked Leroy.

"And *you* get along with everyone?" Elsa snapped.

"Everyone," Leroy agreed. He rapped Freddie on the top of the head. "Freddie and Willie are lucky to have me to keep them popular."

"Huh," said Pauline, who'd been quiet for a while. She shifted her weight from sneaker to sneaker. "Where *is* William? Anyone seen him since this morning?"

"He went out after the announcement," said Freddie. "I figured he'd be back."

"Kind of a dick maneuver," Leroy said. "Invite a fuck-ton of strangers then leave us to deal with them."

Elsa, still wound up, snapped, "I'm *glad* there are new people here. William actually *knows* how to make a splash." She laughed. "I will *never* get over the time he put the alarm clock in Khaleesi's locker."

Leroy laughed too. He tapped his forehead and then gave Elsa a thumbs-up, miming *Great minds think alike*. "Doubtless. I got to see a real life bomb squad."

Pauline made a face. "Yeah, I don't know. She could have gotten arrested for making a bomb threat."

"But she *didn't* get arrested for making a bomb threat, did she? She should have known better than to talk shit about people's girlfriends." Elsa waved off the conversation with a scoff. Her voice suddenly went honeyed. "Hey there, Olivia. Haven't *you* been quiet? You okay? You all there?"

Olivia stirred. She realized she'd been standing for a while now, just listening to them. Their argument sounded like waves, surging and breaking and crashing. Her bottle was empty. Everything was shining, which was either real or because of the drug, the what's-it-called, Angie's bones.

Olivia's hands tensed around the bottle. Talking to Elsa was stressful. "I'm fine."

"How's life at Brown?" Elsa pressed sweetly. "Does Brown *have* remedial classes?"

"I'm not in remedial classes."

"So you're failing out," Elsa said.

The accusation caught Olivia like a blow to the stomach.

Don't think about Brown, Olivia told herself. *Don't think about spring semester starting in ten days. Don't think about telling your parents.*

"Looks like I hit a nerve," Elsa said lightly.

"Whoa," said Leroy.

"Low blow," said Freddie.

Disapprovingly, Pauline said, "Not nice, Elsa. We don't shoot foals."

Olivia felt like she was going to fall down. She tried to make her head come together all in one place.

Her friends had started arguing again, so at least no one was paying attention. The sofa was close by. Someone called something after her that she couldn't make out, so she said, "Just need to lie down a minute," and that seemed to make them stop.

The sofa was so white and soft. The windows so wide, the mountains so vast. The sky like a hug. The trees a crowd of friends, waving. The little blobs on skis shouted "whee!"

This ecstasy she was on was weird. No, not ecstasy. Angie's bones.

Through half a dream, she listened to people return with their contest entries. Voices blended together.

"—and *since* DNA degrades so fast, *Jurassic Park* isn't even *possible—*"

"—so the *hard* part was finding someone who would *sell* me that much coal—"

"—since that girl, what's her name, Eve, won with a piss joke, I started wondering what I could do with crap—"

"—but what'll you do if you actually end up *in* Congress?" "I'll concede to the other guy—"

"—I won't be *destroying* anything. The painting's just fine where it is, where no one will lay eyes on it until

America's some crap you learn about in Ancient Civ." "The full Martin Shkreli." "Who? Why do you always bring up random shit, Freddie?"

"—and I already sent it all to research in astrology. Bam. Done." "Ha. I should have sent mine to the Catholic Church." "It's a rich area. I heard people arguing about whether to donate to the Flat Earthers or Victim Nation—"

"—only four performances, and I bought them all out—"

"—plans to build a beach house in New Orleans—"

"—who's going to decide what's a waste or not? That's what I want to know." "Chappy and Caesar will decide." "Is William doing anything here? Where *is* William?" "Hm. I don't see him—"

Katie asked, "Do you ever feel like everyone you know fits in one dimension, like drawings on a piece of paper instead of people?"

Oh. That last voice was different. It was nearby.

Oh. It was Katie, playing with her ponytail. At some point, she'd come back to the sofa. It was nice sitting there together, facing all those mountains.

Katie said, "I think when we're young like this, we're trying to understand ourselves. We think we have to be only one thing. We try to be it as completely as we can. Don's the charming clown. Elsa's the mean girl. Pauline's sporty and breezy, Freddie's always in his head, Leroy's cock of the walk. And William's *William,* the smart asshole, the one who gets what he wants because he's a *genius* and he's just like that and you *owe the world* to do what he says—" She tugged hard on her ponytail. Breathed a few times. Shrugged. "And you're, well—you know."

Olivia didn't.

Katie sighed. "I was, I don't know—the sidekick, maybe. William's muse. I liked it. I thought I did." She rubbed her face. "I can't default to that anymore when I'm at school. No one automatically thinks that's the kind of person I am. I have to choose who to be—but I don't really have any experience in being honest with myself."

"I know what you mean," Olivia said. "Who are you when no one's around?"

"Yes, sort of," said Katie, looking a bit surprised. "More like—how much of our identities are shaped by the people we choose to spend time with? We mold each other, you know? We push each other into roles, and we take those roles, and we act them out." She paused, thoughtful. "I think part of growing up is growing out of that. I hope it is."

"I just want to come home and go back to who I was," Olivia said plaintively.

Katie looked at Olivia for a few silent seconds. "You

know," she said slowly, "Pauline gave me some Angie's bones."

"Me too," said Olivia.

"I thought so. How many?"

"Just one."

"But you're so tiny. It must have a big effect on you."

"Oh?"

The room was moving toward the mountains, which were waving their trees to ask for company. The room wasn't rushing, just ambling on.

"Are you feeling bad?" asked Katie. She put a hand on Olivia's shoulder. "You need to tell me if you start feeling bad."

"I feel nice," Olivia said.

Olivia waved at the mountains. Katie looked between Olivia and the window with concern.

Olivia said, "I have one B this semester. The professor says I have good instincts. It's just calculus, basic stuff. Numbers are . . . numbers. They stay still."

"College is hard, Olivia," Katie said. "A lot of people have trouble starting out."

"In calculus, you're safe for an hour," Olivia said, distant. "The professor says I have good instincts for numbers. Numbers know what they mean. It's just basic calculus. . . ."

"For two hundred thousand years, not a single person

in the world understood calculus," Katie said. "You know something that no one could figure out for two hundred thousand years. Isn't that incredible?"

"I don't know," Olivia said.

Katie was smiling at her, though. Like the mountains.

Sarah

At first, the sun peered through the clouds like a child peering through the curtains at a dance recital. Soon, it strutted into the open, showboating like it was summer. Occasionally, it got nervous again, and drew the curtain briefly over its face.

The Service Liaison Office echoed with the swish of skirts, hushed chatter, and the occasional shriek of a toddler's laughter. The air smelled of people and air-conditioning.

A lot of women were already on the way home in vans driven by women who couldn't take the protest walk because they were too old or injured. Even with all those women gone, there were still enough left to bustle. Every year, about half the clerks went home as the crowd thinned in the afternoon, so the wait in line for open windows stayed about the same all day. Some women thought it was a scheme to make sure the social workers had time to harass them. Heretical Mormons were always trying to control them with UBI money.

On UBI Day, the office always looked like it was in

the middle of repairs. The kiosks and automated access systems were all pushed against the walls, most with "closed" signs taped over their connecting pads, a few hidden under fabric. Sarah's mom had commented more than once that it was amazing how many things they had to change just to accommodate people who didn't carry machines everywhere.

Clerks' voices blared and muttered. The weird, old audio equipment sometimes made screeching noises out of nowhere, or amplified the sound of someone tapping their finger on the counter until it was deafening. When the clerks lowered their lips to call a name, whether quietly or loudly, it came out fuzzy. It made Sarah feel like she was on the bottom of a bathtub with cotton in her ears.

The cleaner they used smelled like a toothache.

The door opened again behind them. Agnes jolted.

It was the kid who had called to Agnes from the line of protestors. When he saw Sarah, his expression froze. He raised his open palms defensively. "Just here for the bathroom."

Sarah nodded and the kid relaxed. Agnes squirmed as close to Sarah as she could while he walked past.

Sarah turned her head to keep watching him. From the front, he looked distinct, with heavy blond eyebrows and a scatter of moles on his right cheek. From behind, he was a skinny boy in jeans; he could have been anyone.

Sarah called out, "Hey! Do you know my brother Toby?"

She gasped, shocked at herself. What a weird thing to say—

They spoke at the same time:

"I don't think I do—"

"No, of course you don't—"

They cut off. In the uncomfortable silence, Agnes made a noise like a scared lamb and burrowed her face into Sarah's skirt.

"Sorry, I shouldn't have asked," Sarah said. "I don't know why I did."

The kid made a sympathetic face. "It's okay. Sorry I don't know him."

As the kid left for the bathroom again, Sarah glanced quickly around the room to see if anyone had noticed her outburst about Toby. She wasn't supposed to talk about him. What she'd just done was a lot more significant than blurting the story to one little girl on the road. This was an echoing room full of people.

No one was looking in her direction. Maybe no one had heard. Maybe they were saving it to tell Faith and the others. Maybe some of them understood grief.

Sarah guided Agnes to the check-in to enter their names so they could wait to be called.

Voices ebbed and flowed, blending conversations together. Weird, magnified echoes from the old machines mingled with sentences that surfaced and sank like waves through the ocean of sound. *Name and ID, please. Sign here, please. No, I can't reverse the traffic fines—they're applied before the disbursements get to us.*

Patricia Walther, mother of Eden Walther, Nick Walther, Galilee Walther.

A woman in a lavender dress went between groups, addressing individual women in a voice that never quite rose to comprehensibility. She tried to give out glossy brochures and ask the women to put information on her tablet. Most declined politely with a head shake and a downcast look to indicate they did not want to speak further. A few women ignored her, tending to their children to seem busy. One glared fixedly, motionless, mouth determinedly downturned, until the social worker veered toward someone else to avoid a stare-down.

Varied voices from different conversations wove together.

Name and ID, thanks. And sign here. Sorry, ma'am, we need all the paperwork before you can collect for your son in absentia. I'm already churched, ma'am. Is this your current address? Well, hello there! Aren't you adorable? You'd have to ask them yourself, ma'am. It looks like a system error, ma'am; we won't be able to fix it today.

Rejoice Minter and children Matt, Gideon, Young, Char-

ity, and… this looks like it's entered wrong… Bunny? Bunny Minter?

"Excuse me," said a small voice.

Sarah blinked, and realized she'd been too caught up in listening to notice the social worker in the lavender dress had reached her and Agnes. Agnes did not burrow into Sarah's skirt, although she did clutch at her arm.

The woman's perfume was a flowery mix, but none of the smells were lavender. "I have some papers here that outline the social services we're able to provide here," said the woman in lavender. "Of course, you can also ask me any questions. If you will leave your name and information here…" she said, extending the tablet.

Sarah regarded her levelly.

The social worker seemed taken aback and Sarah wondered if she'd gotten past this part of her speech all day. The small woman wore her hair in a loose bun. Her finely drawn brows were slightly raised in surprise.

Her gaze flicked down to Agnes and to Sarah's stomach. She offered the tablet again. "There's a lot we can do for children…."

Sarah gave a wordless shake of the head, but she met the woman's eyes while she did. One was brown and one was blue. She tried to figure out what the woman's expression meant—it seemed like some combination of sad and nervous—and also seeking, as if the woman were trying to figure out what was in Sarah's eyes, too.

The social worker broke eye contact, but murmured as she left, "You can ask anytime."

Sarah realized a pair of women had been watching their interaction. When Sarah looked at them, Rainbow turned away, pretending she hadn't noticed. Mariah, switching baby Ardeth to her other hip, gave Sarah an offended glare.

Name and ID, please. Actually, if you could sign just under that. Ma'am, are you sure you don't need a candy for your blood sugar? Wow, look at your curls! Aren't you lucky? I can ask him to come out, ma'am, but you'll probably have to wait. Yes, your husband is still entitled to UBI as a felon, but we can't do anything until he surrenders. Ma'am, please stop your child from drawing on that!

Mariah Talbert, mother of Justine, Oakley, Ardeth.

Flicking Sarah a final glance of resentment, Mariah pushed her children toward the counter, following with the baby.

Name and ID, please. I'll need you to sign—Oh, I see you're also claiming for your son Bartholomew?

Sarah's head snapped toward the counter.

She remembered the excuse: Bartholomew was listening to outsider music.

All those boys. All those lies like barbed hooks, everywhere.

Do you have his paperwork with you?

"You're squeezing my hand," said Agnes.

Sarah hadn't paid much attention to the rude, fidgety boy before he left. She hadn't thought of him much after he left either—except for the time he'd come back six months ago. He tried to give his mother some money, but she turned her back and refused to talk to him. Sarah imagined her family turning away from Toby, and wanted to scream.

"Sarah," Agnes insisted with a whine.

And under that, you need to list a reason why he can't be here himself.

They'd always claimed money for the exiled boys. It was virtuous to bleed the government beast. Who would be claiming Toby with their mother gone? Ada, her father's oldest wife? Trinity, his newest?

Sarah broke into motion, pulling her cousin behind her. Agnes exclaimed in surprise. "Sarah!" Their footsteps echoed over the voices and the swishing skirts. Sarah grabbed for a little boy's hand, but his mother pulled him back.

Sarah stopped short by the table in back where the woman in lavender was fussing over piles of brochures laid out in rows. The social worker looked up.

Sarah said, "We need help."

UBI DAY: EVENING

Hannah

Over Canastota, the storm stilled. It didn't feel as if it had left; the usual evening wind felt like the storm's resting breath. The dimming sky was slowly turning the same bruised color as the clouds.

Jake and Isaiah were panting by the time they had pulled the furniture away from the door again so they could come out. They emerged, faces shiny with excitement. They hadn't heard what happened—a blessing—but they knew they were being allowed out *on Windfall Day* because they were safe from Mom.

Jake asked five different times in five different ways if it was really okay to go downstairs before he finally believed Hannah and took off with Isaiah in a rushing ball of limbs. Elizabeth, lingering at the bottom of the stairs, cried out a happy greeting. Hannah followed the boys, slowly.

After a few minutes, Hannah noticed that Jake had stopped bouncing around. He was lingering near the bookcases instead, watching to make sure she was okay. Another surge of sadness passed through her as she wished Jake could have a life where it never occurred to him to worry about things like that—but she waved it off. Today, they were safe. Probably.

She couldn't help obsessing about what would happen if Abigail came back again. This encounter would probably confuse Abigail for a few days, but when she didn't find Hannah and the kids anywhere else, she might track back. It seemed likely that the memory of the gun would only discourage her until her pride started gnawing, and then she'd rile herself up by telling herself there was no reason to be afraid of an old lady like Elizabeth.

Jake asked Elizabeth if they could play with the toys she stored in the front room cabinets. Usually they couldn't; it was in the lease. Elizabeth agreed. The three of them unpacked her cartoon figures, and then the boys bolted upstairs to grab their action figures so they could show them off too. When they got back, Elizabeth started a battle royale between Elmer Fudd and Flash Freeze.

Hannah sat in one of the less uncomfortable old armchairs and watched, letting the noise blend into a pleasant slurry. She must have fallen asleep because when she woke up, Elizabeth wasn't in the room anymore. Jake and Isaiah were lying next to each other, intently coloring in books Hannah didn't remember buying for them. Jake was working on a sword-wielding princess from one of the recent Disney movies Hannah couldn't keep straight, and Isaiah was scribbling over an anthropomorphic hammer dancing with a screwdriver. The coloring books looked like they were from Elizabeth's collection. Hannah hoped the boys had permission.

Elizabeth wasn't there.

Hannah leaned forward in her chair. "Did Elizabeth go home?"

Jake startled a little. Both boys sat up to look at her.

"It's a hammer!" Isaiah said, banging his fist on the coloring book page to demonstrate.

Jake shook his head. "No, she went in the kitchen for tea, but she's still there." He paused. "I think she's sad."

Intuition like a heat-seeking missile.

"I'll make sure she knows where the tea is," Hannah said. Her blood pressure spiked at the thought of leaving them, even to go into the next room. She added, "If you hear *anything*, come straight into the kitchen. *Anything.*"

Jake nodded. Isaiah chewed on a crayon.

Hannah touched the mezuzah on the door leading into the kitchen. She entered quietly in case Elizabeth had fallen asleep or was lost in thought. The older woman was sitting on a barstool at the counter, looking at the wall behind the refrigerator, weeping quietly.

Hannah cleared her throat. Elizabeth blotted her tears and turned toward Hannah.

“Thank you.” Hannah had said it before with the boys there, but this felt more personal. “Giving us a Windfall Day where the boys can play downstairs means more than you realize.” She paused. “Did you give them some coloring books?”

Elizabeth looked concerned. “I hope you don’t mind.”

“Oh, no, it’s fine! I just wanted to make sure they had permission.” Hannah glanced behind her, thinking about going back to the boys. “Are you all right?”

Elizabeth nodded distractedly. Her gaze moved to the wall again as more tears gathered in her eyes. “As well as I’m meant to be.”

“Do you want to talk?”

Elizabeth didn’t answer for a minute. Hannah was considering whether this was Elizabeth’s way of asking her to leave when the older woman finally made eye contact.

“Are you still married to that woman?” Elizabeth asked. She saw that Hannah looked taken aback, and added, “I’m not judging.”

“I pushed through the divorce,” Hannah said.

“Oh. Good,” she said with relief. She explained, “I try not to lie. I’ll lie if I have to—but when I keep the truth, I feel like I’m right with God, if you know what I mean.”

“Oh, and you told Abigail you hadn’t seen her wife.” Hannah gave a dry laugh. “I guess you haven’t.”

"I figured even if you were still married on paper, if she treats her family like this, you're not married in God's eyes." She shrugged. "Maybe that's shaky, but I thought it was good enough."

The silence returned.

Hannah shifted uncomfortably. She would normally have left Elizabeth to her privacy, but she had a sense that the older woman wanted her to stay.

"Do you want to talk about why you were crying?" Hannah asked.

"Oh." Elizabeth's face fell. She hesitated. "Yes."

Hannah sat on the barstool beside her.

Elizabeth wasn't crying anymore, but her eyes were still red. "I'm a Christian woman. I want you to understand that."

"I understand."

"They say we're all works in progress, but I work hard to keep right with God. When we were in the army, we obeyed our COs. But a lot of people give God less respect than they give a CO. Now, my parents would have said people like you were sinning. Myself, I think people have to work those things out with God themselves."

Hannah nodded.

Elizabeth looked into the distance again, gaze diffuse. "It was decades ago, before I was in the army. Wayne and I got married before we left high school because our first was well on his way before graduation. That was a sin too, but it was a sin that made our Nathan, so I don't have it in my heart to regret it. We had two more. I stopped working because childcare was too expensive."

She continued, "Wayne had a job at a real, actual factory. There were some left. Ha. But the factory closed and boom. We were two unemployed people with three children, making zero dollars between us. I think that's when I decided I was going to join the army. Took me another eighteen months to do it, but I think that was it. Earn money and protect our country. There wasn't even a risk of going into combat, not that I'd have turned it down. Things are so different now. We were worried about Russia and China and the Middle East. No one was even thinking about India."

She shook off the digression.

"Sorry, it's so easy to get on tangents when you're old. Everything is full of *time*." She paused, realizing she'd done it again. "Or maybe I'm trying to avoid the subject."

She rubbed her face with her hands.

"You can stop," Hannah said.

"I probably should," Elizabeth said. "I'm too old to put my problems on other people. You don't need more to think about."

Hannah hesitated. In general, she did prefer to be left out of other people's business. "I want to know."

Elizabeth sighed again. "So, Wayne's laid off, and there are three children needing food, and, well. I got pregnant."

The older woman swallowed hard and cut off. Hannah shifted on the barstool, not sure whether she was supposed to pat her shoulder or something.

". . . It was so long ago," Elizabeth repeated eventually. "I was—Roe was still national. All kinds of people had abortions. It was *normal.*"

Elizabeth flicked her gaze toward Hannah as if bracing herself for a retort. Hannah kept her face blank. She was *not* going to argue about abortion with someone she hardly knew, especially someone who wasn't Jewish. Every once in a while, Hannah ran into someone who wanted to blame her *personally* for the abortions performed under Jewish religious exemptions. It was always so unbearable that the other 95 percent of discussions weren't worth it.

After waiting a beat for Hannah to interject, Elizabeth continued, "The kids needed to eat. I'd gotten sick with the last one, and we didn't know if it would happen again or what we'd do without any money to get help—" Elizabeth set her jaw. "In the army, you learn a lot about control. Control, discipline, how to keep your head when everything's wrong. I wish I could go back to that time, but I can't."

Hannah nodded slowly. "People do what they have to do."

"When you do something evil, *why* isn't important," Elizabeth said. "There's still evil in the world that you put into it."

Hannah let her disagreement lie.

"So, Hannah," Elizabeth said, clearing her throat. "You have the money to take care of those kids. I expect you to do it."

Hannah replied emphatically, "Oh, I will."

"How often does your ex find you? Does it happen every year?"

"More than that," Hannah said, "but this time of year is the worst. She's obsessed because January fifteenth is when we left. I was opening my check—I got it in the mail back then—and I thought, *Here's something that's just mine, that she can't get to*. It was big enough for me to start my own bank account and put a deposit on a rental house on the other side of the country."

Hannah hadn't meant to reveal so much, but once she'd started, she found she couldn't stop. "We can't settle in *anywhere*. You never know when she's going to find us, or who'll tip her off. People think they're being helpful. My hairdresser accidentally warned me once before Abigail could get to town because he was so excited to tell me about being contacted by my 'estranged sister.' I know why they tell her. Abigail doesn't look scary if she doesn't want to. She's confident, magnetic. Believe me, I know."

Hannah heard her own voice go raw and hot.

"I get so tired," Hannah said. "I just want it to stop. I'm not sure it's going to stop."

Her rant suddenly ran out, leaving her panting and glazed with anxious sweat.

"That's terrible," Elizabeth said.

Hannah shrugged. It was.

"Can your family help?" asked Elizabeth.

"My sib lives in Moscow. We don't have a lot of time to talk."

"Your parents gone? No aunts or uncles?"

"Everyone splintered off. Before I was born, mostly," Hannah said. "Abigail's parents have actually helped us out a couple times, but if we stay too long, they start trying to get us back together. They just don't understand what's happened to Abigail. They think she'll be okay if she has us back. They think she can't start getting better without me."

"Well," said Elizabeth. "Here."

This time, when Elizabeth tugged her sweatshirt out of the way, Hannah could see that the other woman was wearing a side holster over her blouse. Hannah flinched a little, and caught Elizabeth's brief look of exasperation as the woman flipped a hook to release a flap. Elizabeth slid out the gun, detached a metal part, did something to the barrel, and held out the thing to Hannah.

Hannah leaned backward. "Are you giving this to me? Thanks, but no. I don't want it around the children."

Elizabeth gave her a hard look. "Don't give me that after you saw me drive her off with this. You're going to take it, and you're going to protect your children with it until you can get your own."

Hannah stared at it. She intended to say no, but the words changed in her mouth. "Okay."

Hannah accepted the gun. It made a weird weight in her hand. She tried not to jerk away. Guns were supposed to be safe from accidental firing now, but she didn't care what the gun manufacturers said—it was impossible to make a safety mechanism that couldn't fail. She listened with half an ear to Elizabeth explaining where she should go to learn how to use the gun, and warning her not to load in more ammunition until she did. Even holding the gun felt so weird that Hannah didn't really register the rest. It seemed like Elizabeth was involved in teaching for some training program; she wavved a brochure from her phone to Hannah's.

"—and when you've passed all that, we'll rekey the biometrics," Elizabeth finished. She pointed at the window behind the sink. "It's awfully late by now."

Hannah looked up at the darkness seeping through the translucent curtains. “Oh.”

“I need to go home. You have my number. Call if you need anything.” Elizabeth paused. “I’m coming by tomorrow. Don’t tell me not to. I’ll come even if you do.”

“I won’t, then,” Hannah said.

Elizabeth opened her arms and Hannah took the hug. It felt odd to hug another adult. She realized, suddenly, how lonely she was. Even two wonderful, intuitive children couldn’t fill an entire life.

The hug lasted almost two minutes. Elizabeth went into the front room to say goodbye to the children. Hannah stayed where she was for a while, in the quiet.

Janelle

The tense sky gave way to an anticlimactic evening. There was no violent rain, no blasting wind. It began to snow again, lightly but steadily. People's footsteps crunched over the thin layer that fell onto sidewalks someone had cleared earlier in the day.

Janelle slowed down as she entered one of the hospital's waiting rooms, following Nevaeh. Almost every chair was full, but her attention still went straight to her sister, who was sobbing while everyone around her looked like they couldn't figure out how to help.

"Thanks," Janelle said, waving off inquiries as she helped Nevaeh up. "She's my sister. I've got it from here."

Janelle held Nevaeh's hand as they ducked back into the hallway. It was UBI Day at a hospital; of course everything was full. There was a coffee machine in the lobby that was out of cups; Janelle sat on the floor next to it and gestured for Nevaeh to join her.

"Nevaeh," Janelle said. "You did not ruin my life. Why do you think you ruined my life? Did I make you think you ruined my life?"

Nevaeh sat down and wrapped her arms around her knees. "You had a career. You were living in Atlanta. You were doing things! Then you had to come here and take care of me. And you couldn't live where you wanted to live, and you couldn't do what you wanted to do, and you broke up with Andi, and you don't date anymore, and you have to work on stuff you hate. And you used to try to change the world! I took you away from the world. I took the world away from you!"

A pair of impatient white shoes stopped next to them. Janelle looked up and saw they were connected to an impatient White person: a frazzled-looking nurse wearing an excruciatingly adorable panda print on their scrubs and mask.

The nurse pointed to Janelle's buzzcam. "You can't have that on in the hospital." Their voice was crisp; their mask filter was a good one.

"My aggregator arranged a press exception for me to conduct some interviews." Janelle unzipped her purse. "I have it on my phone—"

The nurse interrupted. "Do your interviews, or turn it off. You can't just sit here filming."

Janelle glanced at Nevaeh, who shrugged.

"Want to answer some questions?" Janelle asked.

"I don't have time."

Interior, hospital.

Nurse with cute panda scrubs: No one who works here is going to have time for you today. There, you can call that an interview. [Turning toward Nevaeh] If you need tissues, ask at the desk. I hope you feel better, honey.

Janelle plucked the camera out of the air. The nurse waited for it to go dark before leaving.

Janelle and Nevaeh watched her go, letting the moment settle.

"My life isn't ruined," Janelle said. "It's different than it was going to be. Sometimes, I miss being effective. Not the work, but actually getting something done that mattered instead of just doing the same thing over and over. Then I tell myself, oh my God, how can I forget I'm doing something that matters?"

In a snide tone, Nevaeh muttered, "Children are 'the magic of the future.'"

"Children are obnoxious and full of substances that leak. I'm not raising 'children.' I'm here with *you*. I like hanging out with you. I thought you liked hanging out with me, too."

Nevaeh shrugged. "Why should you have to hang out with some dumb kid?"

Janelle considered what to say next. Nevaeh wasn't making eye contact, but she kept sliding her gaze over to see Janelle's expression.

"Nevaeh, did Mom tell you how you got your name?" asked Janelle.

"She was looking up at a stained glass window in a Catholic church."

"It was a window in a dream, actually. Clever Mom. She was always a good not-quite liar." Janelle snorted. "Mom said that, in the dream, an angel put you in her arms. They'd already mostly raised me. They weren't thinking about more kids. But the angel came and put 'a piece of heaven in her arms.' So she named you Heaven. She changed to calling you the Prince of her heart when they found out your birth-assigned sex, but Nevaeh was the name she dreamed about. She was so happy when you picked it."

Nevaeh shrugged. "Mom always said it would have been my name if I was a girl. I'm a girl, so it's my name. . . . Why didn't she tell me she dreamed it?"

"Mom used to have a lot of dreams about angels and things. They figured out she had epilepsy, and put her on medication right after you were born, and the dreams stopped. It was hard on her—she decided it meant she was crazy. She threw away a lot of stuff like her paintings, and the collection of glass angels she kept in the window."

"I didn't know that."

"She was embarrassed about it. But I know, in her heart, she still believed in that dream."

"I don't really know anything about Mom or Dad," Nevaeh said, distressed. "I was too little to understand them."

"Sure, you were a kid."

"I'm still a kid."

"A *little* kid. Most little kids don't know their parents like that. They're weird giants who get to make the rules."

"I should have known something!"

"Of course you know something," Janelle said. "Tell me about Dad."

Hesitantly, Nevaeh said, "He was a dermatologist. He was married twice, but the first time he didn't have any kids. He didn't have any brothers or sisters, and he was born in Ohio."

"That's all correct."

"Great, so I know him as well as anybody who read his obituary."

Janelle motioned for her to continue. "Keep going. Tell me about sitting next to him. Don't think about it."

"Uh," said Nevaeh. "He had a thick, yellowy smell in the morning that made my eyes water."

"Cologne."

"He wore clothes with lots of buttons. I used to pull

on the buttons when I was really little before I knew not to put everything in my mouth. It made him really mad."

Janelle pitched her voice down an octave. "'Connie, *get* out the *thread*. The baby *ate* my *shirt* again.'"

"Yeah," said Nevaeh, gaining speed as the memory solidified. "Yeah, he sounded like that. His voice went up and down all the time."

"Try Mom."

Nevaeh bit her lip. "She played the piano. We had to keep going to the same church even though we hated it because she was in the choir."

"Soprano."

"She was always swinging me around and making me dizzy."

"You liked it."

"I liked to hear her talk, so sometimes I'd ask her a question and then . . ." Nevaeh blurted out the rest, embarrassed, ". . . just ignore everything but how she sounded!"

Janelle laughed at how contrite Nevaeh seemed. "Mom liked to talk."

Nevaeh paused. She looked at Janelle assessingly, and then down at her hands wrapped around her knees, and then back at Janelle. "I want to see the photos."

Janelle frowned. "The plane crash photos?"

"Yeah."

Honestly, Janelle didn't like to think about the photographs. They were too blurry to feel cathartic, but also too gory for her to forget what they were. "Let's talk about it again when you graduate from high school."

"I'm old enough."

"Hm."

"I'm sixteen!"

Janelle arched both brows. "This is not a winning argument against anyone over twenty-five." She switched to a serious tone. "What I'm hearing is we need to make our insurance pay for us to spend an hour exercising our vocal cords every other week."

"Therapy?" asked Nevaeh.

"Yup."

Nevaeh shrugged. "I did that after they died."

"It's not like losing your virginity," Janelle said. "You can do it more than once."

"Janni!"

"Sorry. The jokes. I know."

They went quiet for a while. Someone stalked near the coffee machine and muttered about cups.

After a while, Nevaeh said, "You know I mean it. We don't have to live here."

Janelle shook her head. "I couldn't afford to keep the

house, but at least I can keep you in the neighborhood you grew up in."

"I don't care. We can go. You can get a job you like better."

"Nevaeh . . ." Janelle made a worried noise in the back of her throat, trying to figure out how to phrase it. "You're only a kid for two more years. I know that seems like forever to you, but it's not. I have plenty of time left to put myself under so much stress that my hair starts falling out again. Right now, I want to take care of you."

"You want to," Nevaeh repeated dubiously.

"Yeah. I do."

Nevaeh tensed up like she didn't believe her.

Janelle leaned in. "I love you."

Nevaeh turned her head away.

"Hey, little girl. Listen to the embarrassing old person. I love you. Believe me yet?"

Nevaeh looked at her feet. "I don't know. Maybe. I guess."

"Well, you guess right." Janelle paused to stretch her back. "I think it's time to go home."

"What about the interviews?"

Janelle threw herself into the characters:

Patient: I can finally afford the thing I need!

Other Patient: Medical treatment has gone to hell.

Nurse: Do you know how many kids I've seen today whose parents *tear up with gratitude* because they can afford medical care?

Other nurse: Do you know how many kids I've seen today whose parents *abuse and neglect* them because they only wanted the extra money?

Pediatric receptionist: Do you know how many kids *I've seen* today?

Doctor: Oh, hello. It's Janelle, right? You were here last year. And the year before that, and the year before that, and the year before that . . .

Nevaeh laughed, quietly but it seemed sincere.

Janelle got to her feet and offered her hand to help her sister up. They walked together toward the rotating door and the dark snow outside it.

Janelle checked the time. "It's getting close to when I need to call Dynasty, but we have time to stop for ice cream first," Janelle said. "I'm sure we'll find some former econ major to interview who wants to demonstrate his UBI theories with sample cups of sorbet."

"Really?"

"It's happened before."

Olivia

The Colorado crowds began dispersing to their homes and hotels. Their tracks etched the emptying slopes. Overnight, the snow would erase them, leaving everything pristine.

Someone's hand was on Olivia's leg. Their face was in her face. Their mouth was kissing her mouth.

"Charming's here, Princess Liv," said Don. "Waaaake up."

Olivia stirred. Don's weight was pressing on her chest. Her neck was crooked. Without really thinking about it, she pushed at him so she could readjust her position, still confused about what was going on. She got enough room to stop her neck hurting. He was in her face again.

His hand moved up. "Loveable Lady Liv, open the throne room, won't you?"

Her neck was twisted a different way now. She was hot and crushed. She needed air, but her hands were pinned between them.

"—the fuck, Don! Get off her!"

There was less pressure. There was air. Breath moved

easily into and out of her lungs.

Olivia pushed herself up. She must have fallen asleep on the sofa at some point, because it was evening now. She tugged down the hem of her slip dress. Last night, white silk had made her feel sexy. She didn't like it anymore.

Don protested, "Katie, what are you freaking out about? Liv and I did this all the time. Right, Liv? She likes it."

"She was whimpering!"

"*Yeah,* she *was,*" Don said huskily.

"Oh, fuck you."

"Get off your broom, Katie," Don said. "You've been acting superior since we got here, like no one can see you staring down your nose at us. You're not better than everyone else because you wrote some paper on Hume's moral theory."

"No," said Katie. "I'm *better* than you because I don't rape people."

Don sputtered. "That's—You—"

Olivia's vision was still a little blurry, but she saw the shape of Don moving toward the shape of Katie.

"Stop!" shouted Olivia.

The blurry shapes stopped moving.

"I don't want you to get hurt." Olivia gestured at the mountains to stop sneaking up on them.

Katie's dress whirled around her legs as she turned to look at Olivia. In a sudden motion, she snapped back to face Don. "Just leave her alone. You can tell she's trashed. Pauline gave her a whole bone—"

"Holy shit."

"—Luckily, it takes a *lot* to overdose on Angie. I've been watching for whiting, but her irises are still clear and it's been a few hours, so it should be fine. But she's been drinking, too. You *know* that. I don't know what's going on, but she's been freaking out all day—"

"Since when do *you* pay attention to Liv?" asked Don. "It's pretty messed up for you to yell at me for giving her a little attention. Everyone remembers how you used to treat her. If she was on fire, you'd have walked by without even bothering to pour out your acai juice."

"Fine." Katie's tone had a sharp edge of resentment. "I haven't always been the person I want to be. Happy?"

"Why could you *possibly* not want to be the person who used to free up equipment at the gym by telling the fat girls they should try bulimia?"

Katie glanced away, not meeting his eyes. "That's *why* I'm trying to be different. I *need* to be better."

"Not planning to get any more baristas fired for sitting down between customers?"

"We *all* need to be better," Katie said. "Haven't you figured it out yet? How *fucked up* we were in high school?"

"Just because *you* were fucked up doesn't mean *we* were."

Olivia's vision cleared more. People had backed up to leave empty space around Katie and Don. Some of them were watching the fight from the edges, though. People did that.

Don asked, "Why did you even come, Katie? *You* decided to fly out here to spend time with us 'fuckups.'"

"I thought—I don't know. I thought. Maybe you'd have changed. I changed." Katie paused. Her tone became urgent. "Something's *wrong.* Don't you feel it? We're all acting like this party is just the usual William—hedonistic, iconoclastic—but he came in this morning looking like *death*. He's been gone for hours. Did any of us even enter the stupid C&C contest? Did you?"

"No," said Don.

"Me either," said Katie, "and you know Olivia and Pauline didn't. Elsa? No way. Maybe Freddie and Leroy—"

"Leroy did," Don said. "But not Freddie."

"Leroy and William. Two out of the eight of us. It's our big reunion and he throws a party that's got nothing to do with any of us, and fills the room with strangers, and disappears. I know he's a fucking *asshole*—"

Don snorted. "At least you're not calling *him* a rapist."

Katie suddenly went red into a rage. "If you're so sure

Olivia was into it, why didn't you ask first?"

"I thought it would be a nice way to wake up," Don said.

"Just what William would say," Katie spat back. "Olivia, was it a nice way to wake up?"

Olivia imagined that if she got up and walked to the window, it would disappear and she'd just walk straight across the sky to the mountains.

"Just tell her you were into it, Liv," Don said. "Get her off our backs."

Someone behind them whispered, not very quietly, "I thought having the girl on her back was the problem."

"This party is *amazing*," someone else whispered back, singsong. "I love when you can drink *during* the show."

Olivia covered her ears. She kept hearing her name. Olivia. Livvy. Liv. Katie and Don were getting louder and louder. She wanted to stop them fighting, except how? Agreeing with Katie wouldn't do it. Agreeing with Don wouldn't do it either.

She put her head between her knees so everything would seem dark and closed in.

More noise, and more voices. A loud, glassy sound rang out on top of the others. Then more voices, and the glassy sound ringing over and over again. A snarl broke through:

"Pay attention!"

The ringing again. The other noises had gotten quiet enough now that she could recognize what the ringing was. Someone was striking a glass with a fork loudly enough to vibrate the piano strings. Olivia pulled herself up again and twisted to look that way.

William was back, standing by the piano bench.

The conversations faded except for Don and Katie. They hadn't paused at all. Both of them were red in the face.

William jumped on the piano bench and screamed again. "Pay attention to me!"

Don broke off first, leaving Katie shouting alone for a few seconds until she stopped too.

William was breathing heavily. His face was beet red and sweaty. He raised the empty wineglass over his head. He'd lost his shirt at some point, and the too-tight vintage jacket was only buttoned once in the middle. The hollows under his eyes still betrayed that he desperately needed sleep, but there was also unstable excitement in his pupils. They jumped jerkily across the room.

"Ladies, gentlethems, and my fellow incorrigible assholes!" William shouted. "The time has come to trade stories of our adventures."

There was some cheering, but not a lot. William's mouth went tight.

"Of our adventures!" he shouted again. There was a

threatening growl in his voice. “Cheer! Applaud! Your fellow warriors deserve your admiration! Try again, my friends in arms! One of us is about to get the Waste Day crown! The moment of coronation awaits!”

A few nervous cheers quickly petered out.

Leroy and Freddie were standing together, close enough for Olivia to watch their faces. Both of them were scared. Leroy more so, but you’d have to know him to tell; he was blustering.

Leroy asked, “What are *you* crowning someone for? It’s up to Chappy and Caesar who wins.”

“Sure, sure, they’ll judge the actual contest,” William said. “But after a long day, don’t you think we deserve to find out who was the victor of our little battle? Who’s going to carry our banner for us even if we lose the war?”

A giggle came from a corner near the window, behind the bunched-up curtains.

William shouted, “*Who the fuck is back there*?”

A couple of heads peeked out, a boy’s and a girl’s. “Sorry,” said the girl, laughing.

Olivia recognized the boy as the one Pauline had pointed out earlier, the one who . . . she couldn’t remember . . . something about popcorn or Pop-Tarts or Pop Rocks.

“Motherfucker,” Elsa called out from across the room. “Can you even get a hard-on if you’re not in public?”

The guy smirked.

The sound of shattering glass made everyone jump. Olivia's head snapped toward the sound. William had thrown his glass to the floor. The person who'd been sitting there rolled away from the shards, arms raised to protect their face.

Katie said coolly, "William, what's going on?"

A grin cut its way onto William's face. "Nothing is wrong! Ladies, gentlethems, asses with holes, I present to you the winner of this year's Waste Day contest!"

He swept out his arm and drew a fancy bow.

"Voilà," he declared as he straightened. His voice was smug.

A few girls Olivia didn't know clapped nervously.

The mood had gone very, very bad. Olivia felt it too, but she wasn't sure exactly what was wrong. William always wanted to be the center of attention. He always told everyone what to do. William got angry, he lost his temper, he broke things—it was normal.

Somehow, it wasn't.

William continued, "Now, you're thinking: How can he know he's the winner when he hasn't even heard the other entries? My friends, you're right. I don't know what brilliant schemes you've put together. However, I am confident that I have won, and I wager you'll all agree with me when I'm done. If you don't agree, please, by all means, come up and show your own presentation afterward. I won't stop you."

William looked slowly around the room, scanning every face. Olivia's arms prickled with goose bumps.

"Well? Aren't you going to ask me how I know I'm the winner?" asked William.

Freddie had moved protectively in front of Leroy. "How."

"I bought this gun."

William drew a pistol from his coat.

There were some screams. People scrambled in panic. Someone was touching Olivia's arm with tense fingers, almost-but-not-quite grabbing her, as if they were getting ready to pull her away to somewhere safer. Their pulse was fast in their fingers. It was either Katie or Don.

William laughed and pointed the gun upward. "Don't worry. I'm not going after a room full of people with a nineteenth-century pistol. It's fine. You're safe. Go back to your seats. I couldn't hit anything farther away than my feet even if I wanted to."

William casually kicked off his unlaced oxfords. They were still shiny. He was barefoot underneath.

Almost everyone went still. Nervously, most of the people who'd moved followed William's instructions, watching the gun as they returned to their places. The crowd stared at the door and at each other, everyone waiting for someone to be the first to try to leave. The hand stayed on Olivia's arm.

William continued cheerfully, "This is from eighteen-fifty-blah. It's just a Colt, but some famous Confederate asshole shot it in the Civil War, so it's fucking expensive. I'd tell you about the famous Confederate asshole, but who cares what happened to his slave-owning ballsack?

"Now," he continued, "you may say, 'William! This is just a gun! How can it win our game?' Let's puzzle it through, shall we? What is UBI?"

No one responded.

"Come on, friends, we attend the most elite schools in the world! We can do better than this."

Freddie replied in a monotone, "It's an unconditional, automatic stipend dispensed by the US government."

William gave a condescending nod as if he were a satisfied teacher. "A little imprecise, but close enough."

Freddie stared back flatly. Leroy buried his face in Freddie's hair.

William looked in Olivia's direction and something like a grin stretched him from ear to ear, all lopsided. It felt like the grin was being shot straight at her.

He continued, "Universal Basic Income is premised on the idea that society owes everyone a living. Or, to put it another way, that people deserve payment for being alive." He giggled. "So, if they're paying me for being alive, then the biggest waste of UBI is to make me—"

Olivia saw him raise the gun to his temple, but it was still shocking: the bone-jarring echo of the shot, the blood blooming on his forehead. People rushed toward him, too late. William's body fell backward onto the piano, playing a grisly discordance on its way to the floor.

Sarah

The weather relaxed into the evening like someone with sore bones relaxing into a rocking chair. Some people sat in their yards; others went strolling down the street, avoiding the earthworms stranded on the sidewalk. Open windows welcomed the smell of a sky washed clean by rain.

Although the lobby of the Service Office was huge and empty, it turned out that the back rooms were small and stuffy. Sarah and Agnes were put in one shaped like a backward L. The woman in lavender offered them wheeled chairs that were set at an old, scratched conference table. The room smelled dusty and stale at the same time as it smelled like bleach.

Someone asked if they wanted something to drink. Sarah remembered someone saying the heretics didn't drink caffeine, and asked for water.

When they were alone, Agnes rolled her chair back and forth for a while to enjoy the novelty of the wheels rattling as they slid across the linoleum floor. She didn't squeak or smile, and after a while, she rolled up to the table and laid her head down on her arms.

Sarah sat beside her in as relaxed a position as she could manage. She realized, as she finally had the chance to rest, that she hadn't been nauseated for a while. Small blessings.

On the wall, an old clock hung beside a normal one. She watched its second hand jerk between numbers: almost to the four, almost-almost to the four, the four, starting toward the five . . .

Someone came in with a scale. They weighed Agnes, and then left and came back with people who muttered over her bony little body. One of them muttered to himself as he looked at her fingernails: "Curved . . ." He held up her index finger to examine it more closely. He muttered to himself again, "Just like a spoon . . ."

Agnes looked spooked. She stared warily at her hand when he released it.

Those people went, and a woman in a cornflower-blue skirt came in to talk to Sarah. Sitting across the table, the new woman mentioned to Agnes, "You know, we've got a box of toy animals and puppets and things over there, in the corner by the shelves."

Agnes ran off to see if they had horses.

"Hi, I'm Dinah," the woman said. "Kaidence asked me to tell you that 'she's so happy you came to her, and sorry she couldn't stay longer with you two.'" Dinah changed tone, indicating she wasn't quoting anymore. "She has her great-grandmother to take care of this week, along with the kids."

Kaidence was apparently the woman in lavender.

Dinah was holding two cups of water, and balancing a Pepsi can in the crook of her elbow. She set both water glasses down in front of Sarah, saying, "That's for you and your cousin," and then set the Pepsi in front of herself as she sat down.

Sarah nodded to Dinah's can. "I didn't think your people drank that."

"Hm?" Dinah raised her eyebrows. "Oh, hardly anyone worries about soda anymore."

The woman cleared her throat to change the subject. She had long hair, blue eyes, and a face that looked like it was already on the verge of freckling in January. Her smile was friendly in a neutral way. She smelled very crisp, like soap.

"I've got some questions," Dinah said, taking a pad and stylus out of her shoulder bag. "I'll take notes, but it would really help me if you gave permission for me to record sound." She tapped her left ear. "I'm partially deaf in this ear, so it helps if I can go back and listen again to anything I miss."

Sarah nodded. "Okay."

"Thank you," said Dinah.

They started out gingerly with small questions—What is your name? When were you born?—as if they were stepping into the shallow end of a pool. Dinah held the same expression through everything, without a twitch of reaction, which was possibly supposed to suggest that Sarah wouldn't be judged for whatever she said, but ended up feeling unsettling.

In the meanwhile, Agnes had laid out some plastic horses in a line. She discussed them quietly with herself, the occasional phrase breaking through. Sarah tried not to laugh. ". . . should *actually* articulate that way . . ." ". . . really that thin, you'd fall over . . ." ". . . can't stand this way because it'll break your back! Guess we need a bone doctor . . ."

Sarah snorted a laugh. Embarrassed, she flicked a glance of apology at Dinah, but Dinah flashed a smile back.

"My littlest memorizes the scientific names of bugs," Dinah said.

Sarah took the interlude to press her own question, lowering her voice so Agnes wouldn't hear. "Someone said she has fingernails like a spoon. What does that mean?"

"Low on iron, I think," Dinah said. "It's a nutrition problem. They found a couple of them, I think."

"Oh." Sarah frowned. She hadn't spent a lot of time thinking about what things were like in Agnes's house.

Maybe she should have.

"We'll get someone to go through the report with you two. There are also some tests we can't do here, so we won't be able to start everything until tomorrow," Dinah added. "It's nothing we can't fix. Just got to get her some pills and the right food from now on."

"Oh, good," Sarah said distractedly, still thinking about how Agnes never played with her siblings. Agnes should have been able to go to someone else's house if she wasn't getting food at home. Why hadn't she? Blinking back into the moment, Sarah registered what Dinah had said. "I mean, *good*. It's good."

"It is," Dinah agreed.

They both paused for a moment. In the background, they heard, ". . . looks alarmingly like mange!"

Dinah suppressed a laugh, and composed herself again. "Do you mind if we go on?"

"No, it's fine."

Dinah looked at her next question, and took a beat. "You're pregnant?"

"Yes."

"And fifteen now." Dinah glanced at the dates she'd noted and mouthed some calculations. "When you conceived, you would have been—"

"Fourteen," Sarah said, "but my birthday was in a week or two."

Dinah paused, expression unchanging, as she took a couple of deep breaths. She continued, "Married about the same length of time as the pregnancy?"

"Yes, in the summer." Sarah shifted uncomfortably, knowing the heretics didn't like this kind of thing. "I got married young."

"Not really," said Agnes from the corner. "Jessilyn was the same age as you, and Missy was still thirteen until May."

"Thank you, Agnes," Sarah said, aggravated. She looked pleadingly at Dinah. "You need to look for my brother. That's why I'm here. They left him somewhere. He's twelve, and he can't take care of himself."

Dinah asked, "What's his name?"

"Toby."

She nodded. "I'll call to see if they've found any lost boys recently."

"They said he didn't do his chores," Sarah said. "It's made-up, isn't it?"

Dinah made an uncomfortable noise in the back of her throat. Her tongue touched her front teeth as she took a moment to consider what to say. "Demographically"—she glanced at Sarah to see if she'd recognized the word, which she hadn't—"in terms of numbers of people, you can't sustain—keep up—having every man marry more than one woman unless you have more women than men."

Dinah paused, her neutral expression unable to hide a hint of wariness.

Sarah frowned. "Why Toby?" she muttered to herself, but she knew the reason. Toby who cried if you made him touch a dead animal, even one you were about to cook. Toby who stopped talking for a week once, just to see if he could, and no one even noticed. Toby whose slippery hands always dropped the ball, no matter what game you were playing.

Dinah asked a few more questions, and said someone else would be there soon. The door clicked closed behind her, leaving nothing but quiet for several seconds. Agnes got up to sit at the conference table.

Agnes had one of the horses in her hand. She saw Sarah looking at it and explained, "Her back's broken. She shouldn't be alone until we can get her some medical attention."

Sarah snorted.

Quiet again.

Agnes slouched over the table, staring down at the horse figurine she held in her cupped hands. Between cracks, where the conference table was polished, the shine reflected her hands and the figurine in a half dozen blurs.

Agnes sniffed. She sniffed again. She raised her eyes toward Sarah with a stricken look. "I don't want to be here."

Frustration surged. Sarah pushed it down. "You know I'm telling the truth about Toby."

Agnes looked trapped.

"Do you want to go home?" Sarah asked.

Agnes's head began to shake, at first slowly and then faster and faster as if she couldn't stop. Fat tears spilled from her eyes and splattered onto her hair.

No longer protesting that she wanted to leave, Agnes said in a small voice, "I don't like it here."

Sarah wrapped her arms around Agnes, who turned into the hug, still clutching the toy horse.

"I don't either," Sarah whispered, rocking Agnes back and forth.

UBI DAY: LATE

Hannah

In the dark, the blizzard returned to full strength, screaming through the streets. Those who could had gone inside, abandoning the town to the storm for the night. It broke trees and downed power lines, causing widespread outages. Luckily, no one died before power could be restored.

Before she went to sleep, Hannah set down the book she'd been reading in bed, and went to check on the boys one last time. When she cracked the door to their room, Isaiah was asleep on the bottom bunk.

The top bunk was empty. She was surprised. Jake hadn't fought going to bed. He'd seemed happy enough to climb up and snuggle with his stuffed giraffe two hours ago.

She shut the door again quietly so she wouldn't wake Isaiah, and went down to the bottom floor.

There were noises in the kitchen again. The shiver in her spine was worried she'd find Abigail, but the rest of her knew it was going to be Jake.

It was Jake. He was standing by the counter with his

back to her. Half the drawers and lower cabinets were open, along with the oven and the microwave.

Hannah rushed in to close the freezer. “Whoa, kid, what are you doing?”

Jake looked up in surprise. An open duffel bag on the floor held all the knives he’d been able to get to.

“Why do you have the knives out?” Hannah was glad he didn’t know how to get to the really sharp ones, which were out of reach.

“I’m going to make Mom stop,” Jake said.

Hannah gasped involuntarily.

Jake said, “You don’t want to keep running.”

“You can’t stop Mom with a knife.” Hannah lifted the duffel onto the counter and started ferrying the table knives back to the drawer. She suppressed a laugh when she saw he’d included a cake server.

“Mrs. Allen said you should use a gun.”

Hannah sighed. Young ears always heard further than you remembered. “Mrs. Allen was very kind to us today, but the way she does things isn’t the way we do things. I’m not going to use a gun on Abigail. I might keep it . . . maybe . . . if there are no bullets . . . maybe it would scare her. . . .”

She stopped. It also might goad her.

“I don’t know what I’m going to do,” Hannah said, “but no one’s going to stop her with a gun or a knife. Do you really want Mom to get hurt?"

She heard quiet sobs in response and looked away from the drawer. Jake had curled up on the floor, snot running down his face.

Between sobs, Jake said, "What if she'd come earlier and what if I'd been down here with Isaiah and what if she hurt us? And it was my fault? What if she hit Isaiah and he died, Mom? What if he died?"

"That's not what happened," Hannah said.

"But what if it was and he did?"

Then I would tear out her heart with my teeth. "Then you would have called for me before that happened, and I would have distracted her so you and Isaiah could run upstairs."

Instead of being comforted, Jake started sobbing louder. "She'd hurt you again. I don't want her to break my rib again, Mom."

"Okay, listen." Hannah sat on the floor beside him. She grabbed a dish towel and took a swipe at his face. "You aren't responsible for any of this. Ever. If she hurts Isaiah, that's her fault. If she hurts me, that's her fault. If she hurts *you*, that's *her fault*. Some of it's my fault too, because it's my job to protect you. No matter what, it's not yours. You're a kid. You're a good kid. It will never be your fault the adults around you are"—*fucked-up*—"full of problems."

Jake didn't say anything. When she patted his shoulder, he didn't respond at all. She recognized his pouting expression as one of Abigail's and felt sad, knowing he would be upset if he knew that.

"You saw what might happen and you won't do it next time," Hannah said. "You're a good kid."

Jake leaned into her. She realized he was already halfway asleep, and held him with her eyes closed, just feeling his heartbeat close to her skin. After a while, she swiped him with the dish towel again and picked him up to carry him upstairs.

She touched the mezuzah on her way into the living room. Elizabeth's coloring books lay spread open on the rug. Hannah whispered to her son, "Don't tell Elizabeth, but tomorrow let's color on the walls."

Jake murmured something back in his sleep.

Janelle

Chicago's night was thick and black and filled with ice. It was oddly quiet; even the sounds of the trains and cars seemed muffled.

Janelle and Nevaeh, full of ice cream, returned home with a few minutes to spare before the call with Dynasty. Their disbursement checks lay on the counter with the other mail. Janelle pulled down the wavve projector over her desk.

"You'll like Dynasty," Janelle told Nevaeh. "She lives in Missouri, off the grid in a little trailer. You should know she was in jail for a while, so be a little careful about what you say."

"I don't have a problem with ex-cons," protested Nevaeh.

"I know, but it's better to be forewarned," Janelle replied. She did not add: *Also, my darling, you have an enormous mouth and an itsy-bitsy sense of tact.* "You should also know she makes bad pots."

"*Bad* pots?"

"Truly bad." Janelle shrugged. "You might see some on

the wavve. It's what she loves. She's really impressive, too, because she somehow never gets better. It's some kind of talent. She can't sell them, so if you visit, you always end up with a pot. I have one around here somewhere."

Nevaeh glanced around the room as if an ugly pot she'd never seen before might suddenly have appeared on top of the cabinets.

The projection fired up. "Dynasty!" Janelle exclaimed.

Dynasty waved at them. She was a muscular woman with close-cut natural hair and a bright smile. "It's good to see your face and know I got through another year."

Wavves showed an illusion of depth, but most people wavved from inside, so all you could see was someone's wall. Dynasty seemed to be standing in a 3-D forest clearing. Behind her, two folding tables and some camping chairs had been set up in front of her trailer. The surrounding trees sparkled with white lights strung on their bare branches. Apparently, the storm had passed by; there was no trace of snow or mud.

"This is my sister, Nevaeh," said Janelle.

"The one you're raising?"

"Yep! She just found a political conscience."

Nevaeh raised a fist. "Power to the people."

Janelle rolled her eyes. "She's joking."

Dynasty raised her fist back. "Power to the people."

Nevaeh giggled.

Another figure came into view, an old man with a pleasant face and a ready smile. He held his left arm at a weird angle, just out of sight.

"You've got someone with you, too?" asked Janelle.

"Grant," said Grant.

Dynasty continued, "I drove him down to pick up his check when I did earlier. We got stuck in a riot. The Victim Nation people came looking to pick a fight."

"Oh damn, I'm sorry. Are you all right?" Janelle took a second look at how Grant was holding his arm. "Grant, is that a broken arm?"

"Didn't kill me. Therefore, it's making me stronger," said Grant, his tone making it clear he didn't want to talk about it anymore. "Do you take basic income, young woman?"

Janelle said, "Yes."

Grant asked Nevaeh, "And you?"

"Sure, I guess."

"Children!" Grant chastised, tsking. He gestured overbroadly for comic effect.

Dynasty exhaled a mild sigh. "He's done this all day. I asked him to stop."

Genially, Grant waved her off. "And I'm not talking to you about it, am I? I'm talking to her." He peered at Nevaeh. "Too young to know about Tuskegee?"

"Um." Nevaeh looked to her sister.

Janelle explained, "The government ran medical experiments on Black men in the middle of the twentieth century."

Dynasty said, "Grant picked up his oobi for the first time this year so he could give it to his daughter."

"She's having a baby." Grant shrugged. "I'm old anyway." He wagged his finger exaggeratedly. "But you're too young to let them track you."

Nevaeh frowned. "They don't—But . . ." She trailed off and glanced at Janelle. "Is that true?"

Janelle made an uncomfortable noise. "There's a lot of private information in the UBI databases. Homeland Security's gotten caught with their fingers in the cookie jar."

Grant looked smug. "Mm-hmm."

"They changed the law to keep them out," Janelle added.

Grant made a scornful noise. "Ha! They care so much about the law."

"I'll give you that one," conceded Janelle.

"Did you have a good day of interviews?" asked Dynasty.

"Define good," said Janelle, and then remonstrated herself for making another joke like that. "No, yeah, it was a good day. Nevaeh went with me. I made her wear a *terrible* shirt. I should get her to put it on and show it to you."

Nevaeh rolled her eyes.

Janelle continued, "She got kicked out of school today for designing a T-shirt that says *Fuck UBI, we want reparations.*" She leaned forward slightly and put her hands to her mouth as if telling a secret. "Don't tell her, but I'm a little proud."

"I'd wear that," said Grant.

Dynasty looked skeptical. "You wear T-shirts?"

"I'd wear that one. Good for you, young person."

Nevaeh looked both flattered and embarrassed. "Nevaeh."

"Good for you, Nevaeh."

Biting her lip as she looked at Dynasty, Nevaeh asked, "If you're an ex-con, does that mean they're trying to take your UBI?"

Dynasty looked surprised for a moment at the question, but she nodded. "They're only going after felons right now. But yeah, they've got an eye on my check." She turned toward the man beside her. "That make you happy, Grant?"

His genial face sobered. "It does not."

Janelle asked, "Do I see you setting up your windfall party in the back there?"

"Yeah, I got started. I hung up the lights and started putting out snacks."

Janelle explained to Nevaeh, "Dynasty was one of the

first people ever to throw a windfall party. She started out in year one. She hosts a potluck every year for her community."

"The pots are mine," said Dynasty. "Everyone goes home with a pot."

"Got to get rid of them somehow," grumbled Grant.

Janelle cleared her throat. "Dynasty, maybe you can help us out a bit. My Nevaeh here's feeling the pain of not being able to fix the world. I've handled mine by—well, by not handling it. What do you do?"

Dynasty paused to consider. "I don't know," she said after a while. "Sometime I decided I'd just fix what I could fix. Otherwise, it stays broken. What do you think, Grant?"

"I think it hurts." Grant laid his hand over his chest. "It hurts more when you're young because you're not used to it, but the hurt never stops. I think you have to *let* it hurt."

Janelle leaned back to look at her sister. "That help at all?"

Nevaeh frowned. "I don't know. Maybe. Yeah. I've got to think."

"More teenagers should think. Then they'd have some practice as adults," said Grant.

Dynasty glanced behind her. The projection showed people arriving with dishes in their arms. Dynasty said,

"Well, my guests are here. Goodbye, Janelle. Was good to meet you, Nevaeh. Hope to talk next year."

"Bye, Dynasty," said Janelle. "Good to see your face another year."

They ran through the rest of the combinations of goodbyes before Janelle shut down the projector and rolled it back up. Nevaeh stood in place, staring at the wall, thinking.

"Well," Janelle said. "What do you want to do? It's late, but not *that* late."

"Um. Maybe you could show me some of those black-and-white movies from the eighties?" Nevaeh suggested.

Janelle tossed her hands upward in aggravation. "They are *not* black and white! Okay. Let me get in my pajamas. I'll be right back."

Nevaeh picked *Flashdance.*

The ice cream had melted in their stomachs by then, so they settled down with a big bowl of popcorn, Nevaeh resting her head on Janelle's shoulder.

The Paramount logo came on, and Janelle fell asleep. Nevaeh snuggled in, feeling the rhythm of her sister's breath as she watched Jennifer Beals ride her bicycle toward distant skyscrapers.

Olivia

Outside, there was a very light snow.

Olivia stared mutely. The world had gone from shine to blur.

The hand on her arm wasn't Katie's or Don's. It was Pauline's. The tall girl had gone completely pale. Some blood had sprayed over the couch. Red flecked her blonde hair. It was probably good it was in a ponytail.

Olivia wondered if she had blood in her own hair, which was loose down to her shoulders. She touched it. She couldn't tell.

Olivia's ears rang. Something flashed in her eye; it was a message from the accountant. Her funds were available.

Pauline withdrew her hand from Olivia's arm. "I'm sorry." Her tone was sincere, but she was looking away, at the wall.

Olivia got up and instantly forgot she'd been talking to someone. The seconds were disappearing as she experienced them. Everything was gone except what she was looking at right now. That, and that grin on William's face the last time he looked at her.

Freddie was holding Leroy. Leroy had curled into a shaking ball. Freddie rubbed Leroy's back and nuzzled his face into his shoulder.

Also, the sound of the gunshot. That, she remembered, along with the grin.

Another noise: Katie screaming, slumped over William's corpse, covered in blood and terrible things, flailing to push away anyone who got close.

And yet another loud voice: Elsa, wavving emergency, spitting words into her phone like projectiles, trying to talk loudly enough for the operator to hear her over Katie.

That weird grin on William's face.

People would be coming. Investigators. They'd want to talk to everyone. Olivia didn't want to talk to anyone. She stumbled toward the door of the suite.

Underneath the edge of an ottoman, Olivia saw William's oxfords. He'd kicked them away so they wouldn't get blood on them.

"'Attention must be paid,'" someone muttered beside her.

Don: she was passing Don. He took her hand to get her to stop. She blinked at him.

"It's a line from *Death of a Salesman* about Willy Loman when he commits suicide," Don said tonelessly.

"William kept repeating. 'Pay attention, pay attention to me.' It had to be on purpose. It was *William.* He set us up to see if anyone would figure out what he was going to do before he did it." His voice rasped and he swallowed. "That asshole."

Olivia nodded. She took back her hand. She started to leave again.

Don chased after her. "Where are you going? You shouldn't go out alone. You'll hurt yourself."

Olivia wasn't cogent enough to do it consciously, but the back of her mind trawled for an excuse. "Someone should talk to the front desk person."

"Liv—"

She went out the door. He didn't follow. She wasn't sure why. After a second, she forgot all about him.

The hotel carpet was scratchy under her bare feet. The elevator floor was slippery. She looked at her face in the reflective elevator walls. Her face looked weird. Not weird like William's. She still couldn't tell if she had blood in her hair.

The lobby floor was cold. It was slippery, too. She walked across it.

"Hey!" shouted the guy at the front desk. "Hey! Stop! It's too cold to go out like that!"

It *was* cold, even though she was still inside. Olivia was aware of every inch of leg her slip dress didn't cover.

The gunshot sounded in her ears. It covered the clerk's shouting.

The cement outside was even colder. Her footsteps crunched the ice as she moved out from under the awning. The cold hurt now, even where her dress covered. Snow melded the silk to her skin.

There was a taxi waiting near the entrance. Emergency vehicles had begun to arrive, casting a red-and-blue wash across everything. It tinted the taxi driver's exhausted face.

Olivia trudged to the taxi through the snow. She rapped her knuckles on the driver's-side window. The sound was like William tapping the glass.

His weird grin.

The driver looked at her. Her expression turned to alarm. She opened the window partway. "You can't be out in the cold like that! You've got to get inside!"

Olivia shook her head. "Important. This is important."

She fumbled with the clasp on her wrister. Her fingers felt big and clumsy. She couldn't get the hook under her nail.

"Miss! I don't want you to get hurt."

The clasp opened. She pulled the bracelet off. Rose gold flashed so that it almost seemed like the butterfly was flying.

"This cost all my oobi last year. It made me seem interesting. I thought that mattered."

Olivia pushed the wrister against the window.

"You can sell it. It's Tiffany, so it's worth close to the same as it was. Take the money and do something that matters. Something that matters to you."

"Miss—"

Olivia stuck her hand through the window. "Take it."

"I don't think this is—"

"Take it." Olivia dropped the bracelet inside the car.

She started toward the lobby.

The driver unbuckled her belt and threw open the car door. She shouted over the roof. "Miss! I can't take this! It's too expensive—"

Olivia paused. She looked back at the driver, but she was really seeing William's grin.

"Don't waste it," she said, and went inside.

Sarah

The sound of rain came in the dark. It was a determined, steady rain, the kind whose rhythm was musical: the pinging drops against the glass rang like chimes through the percussive accompaniment of the rain that hit the ground.

Back home, Sarah's sister-wives were falling asleep to the rain, each alone in her head. One was furious with Sarah. One felt bad for not finding a way to keep everyone sweet—to keep herself sweet. One was stewing over how bad things could get if people decided Sarah's leaving was their fault. They all avoided thinking about what their husband was going to say in the morning.

Sarah was dreaming.

She'd fallen into a fractured, grayish sleep. In the real world, she made a small noise that was sort of like a whimper and sort of like a question.

In her dream: *Her family was crowding the front yard of her father's house. It was night. Her sisters and her brothers were there—and her mother was there too.* Mother's back? *Sarah wondered.* Maybe I just dreamed she died?

The truck loomed over them, out of sight except for its headlights glaring yellow across the world.

Toby opened the gate to the yard. He called, "I brought something for you, Mom." He had something in his hands. Money? He fanned it out. Money.

He was next to them now, holding the money toward their mother. She stared past him. She didn't see him at all.

"Mom?" asked Toby.

She stared.

"Mom? Mom?"

Then everyone was gone and it was only Sarah left with Toby, who was still holding out the money.

She reached to take it, confused. It didn't seem like things were supposed to be this way. As their hands neared, she forgot about the money; she clasped his hands urgently, and it felt like she had him for a few moments, and then she didn't.

Sarah woke to find Agnes's face staring down at hers. Where was she? It was—Oh right, it was a couch in the small waiting room where they'd been left while someone called someone about something. She felt a rumble of nausea, but it faded away.

"You were making a lot of noise," Agnes said.

"Uh?" said Sarah. "Oh." She rubbed her forehead. "Sorry."

Agnes shrugged. "It seemed like you were sad."

"I was dreaming of Toby," Sarah admitted.

"Oh wow."

"I dreamed Mom wouldn't even look at him, but she would never have done that. Never. If she'd been there, she'd have stopped them." Except, could Mom have stopped them? What if she would have ignored Toby when everyone else did? Sarah muttered bitterly, "If she was going to have to turn her back on him, she'd be glad she was dead."

"Wow," repeated Agnes, taken aback.

Sarah wondered if she'd gone too far. She shrugged.

"Are you worried about your baby?" asked Agnes. "That it won't have a dad? I mean—Sorry if I shouldn't—"

"I'm worried about everything," Sarah said.

Agnes considered.

"If you go back to sleep, will you have another bad dream?" Agnes asked.

"I don't know," mumbled Sarah. She realized her eyes had been closed for a while.

"Go ahead," Agnes said. "I'll watch."

A road stretched out in front of Sarah to the horizon. Toby was somewhere nearby. Was he? Yes, he was. It was like an itch; she could feel him. He had to be somewhere. Didn't he? He did.

A voice called for her. Sarah spun toward it, and it was Agnes, running down the road to catch Sarah in a hug around the waist.

In real life, Agnes wrapped her arms around Sarah as she squeezed in behind her on the couch. It was just wide enough for them both.

In her dream, Sarah and Agnes took each other's hands. They held them tightly, looking into each other's faces. Agnes had changed—she wasn't as skinny, and her skin was better, but most of all, there wasn't any cowering in her eyes. She didn't flinch, didn't tense like she might suddenly have to run.

Eventually, they dropped each other's hands and faced the road arm in arm. It was raining lightly; an occasional drop fell into Sarah's hair. There were fields around them, full of long grass that would turn golden in the summer.

However they turned, the road stretched in front of them. Drizzle silvered the distant horizon. The world was endless.

Sarah picked one of the infinite roads and pointed. She looked to Agnes. Her cousin considered, and then nodded.

Toby was somewhere nearby. They'd find him.

She and Agnes started down the road.

Acknowledgments

Thanks to my husband, Michael Swirsky, and my parents, Lyle Merithew and Sandy Swirsky, for enduring patience and support, both material and emotional.

Thanks to my early readers, some of whom helped form the piece from inception, including, though not limited to: Barry Deutsch, Ann Leckie, P. H. Lee, and Nicole Thayer.

Thanks to the many people in my life and outside it who share their struggles with things like domestic violence, assault, and discrimination. Your stories are a gift of clarity and help so many others feel less alone.

Thanks to the people who have written about their experiences escaping FLDS and other cults.

Thanks to everyone working toward financial justice for Black Americans.

Thanks to the people who've mentored and supported me over the years, some of whom are Andy Duncan, L. Timmel Duchamp, and John Scalzi. Thanks to present and past Tordotcom editors and staff for their work on this project and others, including Irene Gallo, Jonathan Strahan, Emily Goldman, and Patrick Nielsen Hayden.

Thanks to everyone who's taken their time to read this book. I hope you enjoyed it.

About the Author

Folly Blaine

RACHEL SWIRSKY lives in Portland, Oregon, where she roams happily under overcast skies with the hipsters. She holds an MFA from the Iowa Writers' Workshop. Her fiction has appeared in venues including *Tor.com, Asimov's Science Fiction* magazine, and *The Year's Best Non-Required Reading.* Her fiction has been nominated for the Hugo Award, the World Fantasy Award, and the Locus Award, and twice won the Nebula Award.